The No-Boys Club

HO CHE ANDERSON

The No-Boys Club

A NOVEL

A GROUNDWOOD BOOK

DOUGLAS & McINTYRE

TORONTO VANCOUVER BUFFALO

Groundwood Books / Douglas & McIntyre Ltd.
585 Bloor Street West, Toronto, Ontario M6G 1K5

Distributed in the U.S.A. by Publishers Group West
4065 Hollis Street, Emeryville, CA 94608

We acknowledge the financial assistance of the
Canada Council for the Arts, the Ontario Arts Council and the
Government of Canada through the Book Publishing Industry
Development Program for our publishing activities.

Library of Congress Data is available

Canadian Cataloguing in Publication Data

Anderson, Ho Che
The No-Boys Club
A Groundwood book.
ISBN 0-88899-322-6 (bound) ISBN 0-88899-321-8 (pbk.)
I. Title.
PS8551.N3456N62 1998   jC813'.54   C98-930204-0
PZ7.A52No 1998

Cover illustration by Mary Jane Gerber
Design by Michael Solomon
Printed and bound in Canada by Webcom

Contents

For Elke,
for Mom
and for Isabelle—
the three faces of Lark.

1 | Lark vs. the Motorboy

S o I'm walking home on the last day of school and who steps out in front of me but the Motorboy.

Argy and Jennifer and me usually walk home together. We're supposed to be best friends. We all live on the same street, just a few houses apart, but for some reason they brought their bikes to school this morning even though I don't have one. And when I asked them to walk home with me anyway, they just giggled like fools and rode off, which is why I have to face the Motorboy by myself.

Don't get me wrong. I'm more than enough to handle this boy alone. But I pity Argy and Jennifer when I catch up with them. You don't abandon your friends, your *sisters*, not for anything. They've got the nerve to desert me and giggle about it, like they've joined some private little bike club and I'm not invited. Well, fine, we'll see who's laughing next time.

Here's the Motorboy standing in the middle of

the sidewalk. I walk away but he hops on that stupid skateboard and speeds up to me. I ignore him but he keeps talking like we're having a conversation. The only thing I can think of to get rid of him, except maybe pushing him off his skateboard, is to flash him my nasty look, which I do, and I mean my *really* nasty look. But you know what he does?

He smiles at me.

I'm making my eyes look as mad as I can. I'm looking like some kind of devil girl but the Motorboy just stands there smiling. I realize I have no choice. I have to talk to him. I can't see any other way out of this besides pushing him off his skateboard, which by now is looking pretty tempting.

"What do you want, *Skip*?" I say. That's his first name, Skip. Sometimes people call him the Motorboy, but don't ask me why. I think Dumbo would be a better name with those big stupid ears of his.

"I said, what do you want, Skippy Stinkyhead?" I try to sound even madder than I really am.

Skip says, "I just want to talk to you, Lark."

That's my name, Lark. Lark *Farragut*, actually. Okay, Lark *Dorcas* Farragut. It wasn't my idea. My mother named me. She's from Guyana. She says those are the kinds of names they give their children over there, so don't blame me. I think it's a stupid name. Farragut sounds like for her guts, and Dorcas sounds too much like dorkass.

But at least my name's not Skip.

I say, "I don't think you have anything to say to me I could ever be interested in."

Skip says, "How do you know that unless you talk to me?"

"Well, what do you want to talk about?"

"I want to talk about why you're always so mean to me."

"Because you're an idiot." I can say things like that to boys. You know, stuff other boys could say and then get punched in the face over. I can say that because I'm a girl.

Skip just laughs. "How do you know I'm an idiot if you won't talk to me?"

"'Cause I see how you act in school. Always talking back to teachers and walking through the mud and burping and fighting. Every recess I see you fighting with someone. What's your problem? I bet you didn't even pass this year, did you."

"Of course I did," the Motorboy says. Then he

fishes out a crumpled envelope from his backpack and holds it up to me. "See, I even got my report card right here, look. I bet *you* didn't pass."

"I did so!" I start walking again but Skip's right there beside me.

"What are you in such a rush for?" he says.

"I gotta get home."

"Why? What's going on at home so special you gotta rush off for?"

"None of your business. And stop following me. You can't walk me home."

"Who says I want to walk you home? Even if I did I wouldn't walk. I'd take us there on my motorcycle."

I look at Skip the Motorboy sliding along beside me on his skateboard and suddenly I'm really mad. What kind of fool does this guy take me for? Every day he tries to convince me his skateboard is a motorcycle. A *motorcycle,* of all things. Please, do I look that stupid? Does he really think I can't tell the difference between a motorcycle and a skateboard?

So I say that to him, and then I say, "And what's with your name? Who goes around calling themself the *Motorboy?*"

"They call me the Motorboy because that's

what this is. It's not a skateboard, it's a motorcycle."

He gets off his skateboard and holds it up to my face so I'm staring at a little picture of a turtle riding a motorcycle on the bottom. In my mind I'm watching Skip the Motorboy being chased down the street by this turtle. Here's Skip skateboarding for his life and I'm sitting on the grass laughing my head off as this crazy turtle closes in for the kill.

I say, "You know, just because there's a *picture* on your skateboard of a motorcycle doesn't actually *make* it a motorcycle."

Skip shrugs and looks at me like I'm a retard. He says, "Obviously you don't know anything, but that's your problem, not mine."

"No, *you're* my problem."

"No, you're *my* problem."

"If I'm such a big problem why won't you just stop following me? Besides, how're you gonna give me a lift on that skateboard—"

"Motorcycle."

"—*skateboard* anyway. It's too small. It can barely hold *you*." Which is the truth. Skip's not fat or anything but he is really tall. I remember the first time I met him. I saw Jennifer and this group of girls in the park. They were giggling over these goofy tricks Skip was doing on his skateboard. I asked what was so funny, just this dumb boy on his board, big deal. Then Skip looked at me with the same dumb grin he's giving me now and made what *he* thought was a joke, about how since I was so short and he was so tall that all he had to do was lift his leg up and he could step right on my head. And then what happens? He lifts his leg up and tries to do it!

So here we are now and Skip says, "Get on the back and put your arms around my waist, or you can stand on the front and I'll put my arms around your waist so you don't fall off. I'll get you home in no time."

All it takes is one second for me to realize Skip is out of his mind if he thinks he's getting me to put my arms around *him*, or worse, for him to put his arms around *me*. I don't know where he's been. He doesn't look like he knows how to *spell* bath, forget about getting in one. And all I need is for Jennifer or Argy or any of the girls to see me with this guy. I'd never live it down. My life would be over.

I tell him, no way—maybe sounding a little more mad than I really am—and then Skip the Motorboy says, "You want to know what *I* think, Lark? *I* think the reason you're getting so mad is because you *like* me so much. My mother told me that when she was little sometimes she would chase boys around and call them names and stuff, but the only boys she ever did that to were the ones she had crushes on. So I think you really like me but you don't want to admit it and that's why you're getting so mad at me when all I'm doing is trying to talk to you."

Okay... I know boys can be sorta stupid...

And I know probably Skip is just trying to get me mad...

But *nobody*, especially not this big-eared grinning moron, has the right to say to me what he just said.

His mom told him that, did she? Well, I remember a story my mother told me from when she was a little girl in Guyana.

They were by a river where they used to swim after school. My mother was talking with her friends, just minding her own business, when one of the boys came up behind her, and when she turned to tell him and his friends to get lost, he kissed her full on the mouth right there in front of everybody. They were all laughing at her, at *my* mother, because of this boy, she calls him the Phantom Kisser...

But you know what she did? Later on they were all splashing around in the water and my mom swam up behind the Phantom Kisser when he wasn't looking and pulled his bathing suit off before he knew what was going on. Then she got out of the water as fast as she could and hid the thing in the bushes. The Phantom Kisser didn't come out of the water for a whole hour, not until his mother came along and forced my mother to give him back his shorts, and when he finally did come out of the water he was all shriveled up like a prune.

So I look at Skip the Motorboy's big grinning face and his long skinny legs and those big dumbo ears and I think of my mother's adventure with the Phantom Kisser, and even though I want to push him off his skateboard–sorry, *motorcycle*–before I even realize it I'm pulling his pants down and running away and laughing because now there's a big group of girls standing around watching him try to get them back up.

2 | The Party

I think I'm the only person I know who'd even dream of a stunt like the one I just pulled on Skip. I guess I have to finally admit to myself that I am amazing. There's nothing I can't make a success once I put my mind to it. Maybe it's my destiny to be one of the rulers—no, leaders. I have to lead the fight against the nasty stuff in this world. Nasty stuff like Skip, for example, that boy who right now is hopping on his skateboard trying to escape that group of girls.

Maybe he can run but he sure can't hide.

Sometimes I wonder what the world would be like if there was nothing but girls. I wonder if it would be a better place to live. And then I think, *of course* it would.

But then I wonder, if women were the rulers of the world, would everything change or would everything stay pretty much the same? And if things got better, how would they get better? No more Motorboy Skips, that's a pretty good start.

No more fart jokes and making fun of everybody and all that aggressive behavior.

Even my mother says that if women were the leaders, the world would be a better place. She must know what she's talking about, right?

◆

When I walk in my house and everyone jumps out from behind the walls and the furniture and yells, *"SURPRISE!"* I try to act surprised but I don't know how well I pull it off because I knew it was coming.

After I pulled down Skip's pants and began walking home, I started thinking about those girls standing around him, how I'd feel if it was me getting laughed at like that by a bunch of boys. I kept wishing Argy and Jennifer were there to see the whole thing, imagining their faces, mouths wide open, pointing at Skip on the ground. But no, they had to take off on me. Why would they do that? We hadn't had a fight or anything. We walk home from school together pretty much every day, especially on the last day of school. The routine is we walk home and after they drop their report cards off they come to my house and then we all pile in the car and my mom drives us to McDonald's for my...*party*....

Now why didn't I see that coming?

See, for me the last day of school has always been really special. It's the last day of school, yeah, but it's also the day of my birth.

Today I am ten years old.

Well, actually, my birthday doesn't always fall on *exactly* the last day of school but that's the day we always celebrate it. Knowing this, there's no way my friends would just take off on me like that—not unless they were planning something.

My brain started working. Had they been avoiding me today? They'd definitely avoided talking about my birthday. I barely got a "happy birthday" from either of them.

And here I am at home now trying to act surprised at all these people jumping out and yelling for all they're worth. I even jump a little 'cause I think it'll look convincing, but I'm acting and by the way my mom's looking at me with that grin of hers, I think she knows it.

"HAPPY BIRTHDAY TO YOU, HAPPY BIRTHDAY TO YOU, HAPPY BIRTHDAY, DEAR LAAAARRK! HAAAA-PPY BIRTHDAY TO YOU! WHOOOOO!!!"

I'm not surprised but I am happy. Look, everyone's here. There's Shelley and Andrea and Belinda. Mary's here, Robin, Alice, Laura, Xan, Tanya. Tanya even brought her stinky little brother Sheldon and his pal Raymond, but that's okay, we can squeeze them out later. And, ah, yes, there they are, the little Judas sisters, Argy and Jennifer.

Now Mama grabs me and hugs me, saying, "Happy tenth, Baby Lark. Hey, sorry, kid. Ronald McDonald wasn't home this afternoon but I hope this'll be good enough for your majesty."

I hug Mama back hard. I'm so excited I can't say a thing. I'm just standing there with this big stupid grin on my face, but I don't know why. I mean, when I opened the door I knew they were going to do this. It's not like it's a big surprise or anything.

"Hey, Lark."

"Yeah, hey, girl."

It's the bicycle twins, Argy and Jennifer.

"You guys think you're so smart," I say, trying to act mad. "You just took off on me. I thought, what is going on? Did we have some fight I didn't know about? I was getting ready to go to war or something."

They both giggle and Argy says, "I'm sorry."

Jennifer says, "Hey, don't blame us. Wasn't our idea. Your mother planned the whole thing."

"Didn't take much to get you to go along with it, I see." This is my big comeback. I start laughing. I can't even pretend to be mad at these two.

◆

The party's over now, but Argy and Jennifer are still here. It's our birthday-night tradition: the party, and then a sleepover at the birthday girl's house.

Mostly I had a great time. My mother can be *so* sneaky. I think that must be where I get it from. Turns out she was planning the party for a month and she never once let it slip. As soon as they finished yelling *"SURPRISE!"* Mama wheeled out this huge cake she'd made. It was beautiful. It had a vanilla layer between two chocolate layers, and on top she put little marzipan flowers surrounding a little marzipan girl that I think was supposed to be me—glasses, freckles, the whole nine. My mother's amazing!

I started drooling when I sat down in front of all my presents. I got this Lego System Aqua Playscape, a Petite Miss Designer Make-Up Set, a Sailor Moon View Master, Fisher Price Easy In-

Line skates (which were too big for me), and to top it all off, from Jennifer and Argy I got not only Sparkle Beach Barbie, but also the Barbie Sports Cruiser! These are serious gifts. I knew the divas wouldn't let me down.

Of course, I did get some other stuff: soaps and lotions from the Body Shop, some T-shirts and clothes, a collection of Guyanese kid's stories, some okay tapes and this Winnie-the-Pooh coloring book.

And there was this girl at the party—Rena Petzki. Me and her have had this rivalry since we were in kindergarten. She's always gotta show me up. She's always gotta be the first one to have *done* something, to have *seen* something, to *own* something, and she's gotta let everyone know.

Every time I opened a present, the first thing out of her mouth was, "I got that already." "I got that last year." "Oh, that's so old, Lark, I had that when I was a baby but I threw it out."

To listen to this chick, she's owned everything that's ever been invented before anybody on the planet. When she said it after I opened my In-Line skates, that was one thing. Even when she went on about getting the Barbie Sports Cruiser a whole year before me, I stayed calm. But when I opened my Winnie-the-Pooh coloring book and suddenly she's going off about what a dumb gift it is 'cause only babies are supposed to like Winnie-the-Pooh, for some reason I lost it. I don't even like Winnie-the-Pooh, but I stood up, reached for a chunk of my mother's wonderful cake, now an assault missile designed for maximum embarrassment for Rena and maximum satisfaction for me after drilling it at her fat face—

But before I had a chance to throw it, my mother stepped in and pulled me aside.

She said, "What were you gonna do, throw it at her head?"

"What'd it look like?"

"Because you're upset I'm going to let that tone of voice go by," she said. "You know, it's not cool to throw stuff at people, you could have hurt her."

"Yeah, people have died from being hit by cake."

"You know, Lark, you're not too big for me to put you over my knee," my mother said. I couldn't tell if she was mad at me or not. Her voice sounded serious but her face looked playful. I hate when she does that. I can never tell if I'm gonna get it or not.

So I decided to play it safe. I said, "I'm sorry, Mama," not really meaning it.

My mother looked at me and then laughed. I started laughing, too, not because I knew what the joke was but because I was happy to not be in trouble, and because I love to look at her face when she smiles or laughs.

Mama took my glasses off and tried to put them on her face. Too small. She said, "I suppose I can't get too mad at you for something I would have done myself. That Rena's some kind of stush, isn't she?"

"I'll say," I said, happy now because I had my mother on my side again.

"By the way, Ms. Thing, how did you know about this party?"

"What do you mean, Mama?" Playing it dumb again, putting on my sweetie face and my cutie voice, hoping to get out of it.

Mama smiled, not fooled. "You're just like your father," she said.

"I'm just like *you*, Mama."

Beside the dining table where we were all sitting, there was a sideboard that had all the birthday stuff set up—extra napkins, the lootbags my mother was going to hand out, my presents, the remainder of the cake, and some balloons my mother didn't get around to blowing up.

Xan reached over and grabbed a balloon. I had just enough time to look up and see her trying to blow into it before it came flying out of her mouth and hit me right in the face.

I didn't even feel it. I was so shocked I just kept seeing the balloon flying through the air and slapping me in the cheek. People around me were laughing, and just as I went to get a balloon of my own another one sailed across the table and nearly knocked the glasses off me.

That was all it took. I grabbed a handful of balloons and let fly. I was blasting everyone—Xan, Jennifer, Tanya and her stinky brother Sheldon. In a minute, everyone had a balloon and was shooting it at somebody. It was a total war.

When my mother ran in from the kitchen, she shut us down quick.

"HEY!" she yelled, and we just froze.

The balloons flying to people's heads stopped mid-flight and hung in the air waiting for her okay to keep going, but it never came.

Instead she said, "If you kids want to carry on

like a bunch of schoolchildren I can make arrangements to have you all sent back to school for the *entire* summer! If you so need to make noise, don't do it at the table. Go out in the backyard and run around in the sprinkler or something."

So we did. I guess a lot of the people at the party had an idea that something like the sprinkler would happen because almost everyone had brought a bathing suit. There we were, that birthday sun blazing down on our heads, running through that big sprinkler and giggling for all we were worth. We ran through the sprinkler two at a time, did cartwheels over it, stuck our bums into the water to see who could take it the longest. We were having a great time, even the boys, which surprised me 'cause most of the time they act like they're too cool for baby stuff like that. I guess you can imagine what it was like with the boys. A lot of putting their hands in their armpits to make that fart sound, and laughing every time one of the girls fell down on the grass, like they were so superior to everyone. But a couple of jokes about how ugly they were and what girl they think would ever want them, and they shut their stink mouths right away.

It was the middle of the party when it happened. You know that time when you're with your friends and you sort of forget everything and all you can even think about is how much fun you're having? You're laughing and you lose track of time and it doesn't even matter anyway because that moment's never gonna end.

It was after the sprinkler and we were back inside. A bunch of us were sitting in a group in the living room giggling and the guys started to drift near to where we were. So now there were two little groups sitting right next to each other, separated by about four feet. Girls vs. boys. In our group it was me, Argy, Jennifer, Xan and Tanya. In their group it was Tanya's stinky brother Sheldon, Raymond, this guy Jeremy we know from school and this other guy we call Robby Roastbeef 'cause of this one time when he was horsing around during lunch right in front of the principal and dropped his roastbeef sandwich in dog poo and the principal had him sweating by threatening to make him eat it anyway. Argy would never admit it but she has definitely got a crush on Robby Roastbeef. The way she acts around him, all moony-eyed and giggly, it's pathetic.

So one of the guys said something and we said something back and before you knew it there we were sparring with them and I have to give them credit, they weren't backing down.

I sort of remember hearing the doorbell go off and wondering who it could be because all my friends were around, but almost as soon as I thought that I forgot it. I was too busy watching Argy drooling over Robby Roastbeef, laughing about the stuff I was gonna bug her about later.

I heard my mother call out to me, "Lark, another of your friends is here."

I looked up—and saw the Motorboy walking up to me.

◆

"I couldn't believe when I saw him walking up to you, Lark." This is Argy speaking.

Here we are, the three divas camped out on the floor between my bed and the dresser. Jennifer had the bright idea to make a fort, so after we made the floor all cozy with our pillows and blankets, we got two chairs and spaced them out about six feet. Then we draped a couple of blankets over the chairs, the bed and the dresser, and then we draped two towels over the end near the chairs to act as a door. Once we'd brought my lamp in with us and grabbed what was left of the munchies from the party, we were all set.

Getting all snuggly under the covers, I say, "*You* couldn't believe it? How do you think *I* felt? When I saw the Motorboy there I nearly died. Who the hell does this guy think he is? I mean, I can't just let him get away with crashing my party, can I, girls?" I think the answer to that question is obvious. *NO*.

Jennifer says, "Well, what can you do? He already crashed it, Lark."

"Yeah," I say, "but how did he know about it in the first place?"

"Well, Skip's friends with some of the guys that showed up. Him and Sheldon hang tight sometimes. Maybe he told him."

Argy says, "Did you *really* pull his pants down, Lark?"

"Just like I told you, girls," I say proudly.

"I thought there was going to be like the WWF between you two or something, the way you were looking at him, Lark, but then nothing happened. I thought you were gonna try and throw him out."

It's true, I did want to throw him out, but he got to my mother before I could even try. He's there sucking up to her like that Eddie Haskell guy in *Leave It to Beaver.*

"My mother actually came up to me later and told me she thought he was charming and didn't I think he was *cute?*" I almost yell. "Can you believe that? It's like she wants him to be my boyfriend or something."

Jennifer says, "I don't know. What's wrong with that?"

Did I just hear her right? *"What?* What are you talking about?"

Jennifer says, a little afraid, "He doesn't have *cooties* or anything."

"No, he's just got serious boy germs."

Jennifer says, "I think he's kind of cute, the way he sails around on that skateboard."

"Jennifer, how can you say that? Has he ever tried to tell you his skateboard's a motorcycle? What's that all about? Man, I can't believe I'm hearing this from *you* of all people."

"Why do you hate him, anyway? Did he do something to you?"

"Yeah, he was born." Good one.

"C'mon, Lark."

"I don't know. Just *'cause.*"

"Just 'cause *why?*"

She's starting to smile now like she thinks she's got me but I blast her back by saying, "*Because*, he's just so...so..."

"Just so *what*?"

"He's just so *stupid*, okay?!" Man! I'm getting mad now. What does she want me to say? Now she's *really* smiling. Even Argy's getting into it, both of them ganging up on me.

"Oh, yeah?" Jennifer says. "Well, you know what *I* think? I don't think you hate him at all. I think you *like* him."

"*WHAT*?!"

"I think you like him or else why won't you tell me why you hate him? Why are you getting so upset?"

"Shut up."

"*Lark likes Skip, Lark likes Skip—*"

"I do not, Jennifer. Shut up, stop it—"

But she won't stop. She's on a roll now, so I reach inside myself and gather all the force I can and focus it into one of my don't-mess-with-me stares which I level right at her.

I quietly say, "You'd better stop that, Jennifer. I'm not kidding."

Jennifer stops. It looks like she's thinking about

saying something more...no, she's backing down. To tell you the truth I'm relieved. Something's bugging me about this whole Skip thing. Why does she find him cute? All I know is that I don't want to talk about him with her or anyone.

After a minute, Argy, still grinning a little, looks at Jennifer and says, "Do you really think he's cute?"

"Who, Skip?" Jennifer asks. "Well...yeah, I guess." Then she giggles, trying not to.

Argy asks, "How cute do you think he is?"

"I think he's...very cute."

Then Jennifer looks in my direction for a second as if to see how I'm going to react, but I've got my stone face on.

Argy asks, "Oh, yeah? Would you kiss him?"

Stop it...

Jennifer answers, "Maybe."

Argy asks, "Oh, yeah? Would you kiss him on the lips?"

I don't want to hear this...

Jennifer answers, "Maybe."

Argy asks, "Oh, yeah? Would you *tongue* kiss him?"

Arrggghh! "I can't believe I'm hearing this conversation!" I growl. Turning to Argy, I say, "And you, talking about *tongue* kissing, *ooooohh*, would you do that with Robby Roastbeef? Everyone knows you like him."

That got her, but she manages to stammer, "I do not like Robby Roastbeef!"

"You do so. Even Jennifer knows you do. Just ask her." Jennifer giggles and then buries her head in a pillow.

Ending it, I say, "Look, I really just don't want to talk about boys any more. I'm tired of talking about boys, boys, boys. This is my birthday and I say we don't talk about them any more, okay?"

But I can tell they want to keep on talking about them. What's with these girls? Do their whole lives revolve around boys and talking about them? I gotta toughen 'em up. You know what I'd really like to do? I'd like to create a special little place where they wouldn't feel like they always had to think and talk about nothing but boys.

3 | Days of Laze

Ah, summer time...
You know what I've done for the last week since my birthday? Go on, take a guess.

Hey, that's right, I've slept late pretty much every morning, lazing around until I good and feel like getting up, and when I do manage to drag myself from the comforts of my bed, I spend most of the day watching TV.

I love the summer. I don't even have to wait until Saturday morning to watch my cartoons.

Yeah, yeah, yeah. I can just hear you going, what a waste of a perfectly good summer. Little Lark shouldn't be camped out in front of the tube rotting her brain, someone tell her mom! Whatever, you might even be right, but for now I'm gonna let myself get stupider watching this episode of Star Trek.

I see it like this. I work real hard all year at school so I think I've earned the right to do absolutely nothing if I want to. Hey, it's not like I plan to spend the whole summer like this. I just want to watch TV for a little while, catch up on what I missed during the year. Usually what happens is I wake up in the morning and start watching cartoons but just as I'm getting into them I have to get dressed and go to school. Lunch time, same thing. I'm just getting into Sailor Moon and I have to leave again before she saves the world.

A couple of times my mother's gotten really frustrated with me watching so much TV. Now I have to get sneaky about it, what with her pestering me about going outside or picking up a book. She's reaching the breaking point now, I think, so that means some time soon the good life has to come to an end. My mother's on vacation now, managed to get the whole summer off this year to spend with me. When I was really little and my parents lived together, I'd always have someone around to take care of me, but since my parents split up, most years Mama gets a couple of weeks off in the summer and the rest of the time it's either babysitters or day camp hell. I hate day camp. It's exactly the same as school. You get up early in the morning and you stay there until your mom comes to pick you up at the end of the day. No TV, no friends, no fun.

Sometimes I get to spend time with my father. But usually he's pretty busy.

So here I am, 10:03 on a Tuesday morning, watching TV from the comfort of the La-Z-Boy in the living room, still wiping the sleep out of my eyes because I've only been awake a half hour. My mother's outside working in her garden like she does every chance she gets. She's a real out-doors woman. I think it comes from spending the first ten of her twenty-six years growing up in Guyana, deep in the country. I think also the fact that she works as a nurse in a hospital all day, people dying all around her, she just loves to be outside with her growing plants and flowers whenever she can.

I love to watch Mama out there working in that garden. She loves it so much, she makes me love it, too. She gets so excited when she sees a plant or whatever, something she's worked on starting to come to life, she gets all—

Uh-oh, here she is, coming inside. What, did she forget something?

"No, I'm just taking a little break," she says. "Came in to get a drink, relax."

She kisses me on the forehead and then goes to

the kitchen to get a drink before sitting down on the couch across from me.

"What are you watching?" she asks.

"Star Trek," I say. "It's the one where they wind up in that different universe and there's another Spock and he's evil and has a big ol' nasty goatee."

"Yeah, I remember that one," she mumbles. "Shouldn't you be outside enjoying the summer?"

Right on cue. I explain my idea to her about how hard I work during the school year and don't I deserve a break and she says, yeah, I forgot what a tough life you have, Lark, saying it like she doesn't believe me. I guess she's forgotten the dangers of the classroom.

I say, "How are things going with the garden, Mama?"

"So far so good," she says. "Mostly I've just been pulling weeds. After I finish this drink I'm going back out to finally plant that second apple tree. You know, you could help, Baby Lark."

"What could I do?" I say, hoping she won't be able to think of anything.

"Well, you could help me mix the bone meal up with the fertilizer. I need to–"

Saved by the bell. The phone rings at just the

right moment. As I wipe the sweat from my forehead, Mama gets up to answer the phone in the kitchen down the hall. I'm trying to concentrate on evil Spock trying to kill good Kirk, but I can hear my mother on the phone.

"Oh, hey," she says, sounding a little bit, I don't know, mad or maybe just...mad. I'm about to turn the volume up but then I hear her say, "How you doing, Arthur," and right there I'm hooked.

Arthur is my father.

We see each other for a weekend at the end of each month. Sometimes my mother lets me stay a little longer, but that's basically it. My father doesn't call that often, maybe only once every couple of weeks. He used to call more but he stopped. Every time I see him I keep meaning to ask why, but I always forget. Now every time Mama and Daddy get on the phone this is how the conversations seem to go, her answering the phone and right away sounding like she doesn't want to talk to him at all.

Mama says, "No, I'm not trying to start a fight with you, Arthur. I'm just asking you a simple question. If you don't feel you can answer it, then don't start acting like I'm the one picking the fight."

Yeah...it's always the same thing. What are they

talking about that Mama could be getting so upset about?

"No, that's not what I sai...Arthur, all I'm trying to find out is why it is you call your daughter so little," my mother almost yells.

She starts to say something else but stops. There's this silence for a second and then Mama slides the kitchen door closed. I guess I'm not supposed to be hearing this conversation.

Yeah, right.

Silent as a cat, I slink off the La-Z-Boy, glide down the hall and sit on the floor against the wall where my mother can't see even if she opens the kitchen door suddenly.

Through the door I hear her say, "Oh, don't give me that garbage, Arthur. Look, personally I don't care if I never speak to you again, but I'm trying to think of what's best for my kid here, and she seems to think it's talking to you. She'd like to keep in closer contact with her father. Don't ask me why.... Oh, come on! Look, the last thing I'm trying to do is stop you from talking to your daughter. You can call here any time. Don't blame it on me. Arthur, you couldn't even pick up a phone and give Lark a call on her birthday. What's that all about?...Oh, man, that is one lame excuse. You sound like an idiot, you know that? What's with you men?"

I listen for a few more minutes, but soon I start to get upset. I don't want to hear my parents arguing about me. She's saying he's a sucky father and he's saying whatever it is he's saying, and now I'm starting to think maybe if I wasn't here they wouldn't have anything to fight about. Maybe they could still be married or at least still be friends. Maybe if I was a better daughter my father would want to call and talk to me more often and then my mother wouldn't have to yell at him all the time.

I get up from the floor and walk toward the stairs, when I hear the door slide open and my mother call out, "Lark!" I walk back to the kitchen and my mother says, "Hurry up, your father is waiting," saying it like she's ready to kill someone, walking out and not looking back.

I take the phone. "Hi, Daddy." I try to sound like nothing's wrong.

"Hi, Lark," he says. "How are you, baby?" I say I'm fine. He says, "Girl, I'm so sorry I couldn't call you on your birthday. I wanted to so badly, but I was out of the country on business. But I want to make it up to you. I want to do something extra-special with you the next time we're together." I like the sound of that and I ask him what he's got in mind but he won't let on, saying, "Now how am I gonna sit here on this phone and ruin a surprise for my own daughter?"

We talk for a while longer. He tells me about what he was doing out of town, which was playing music. My father's a musician. Mostly he's what he calls a session musician. He sits in a studio and plays music on people's CDs and sometimes for commercials and stuff but other times he plays in concerts when a jazz band needs an extra musician. Sometimes he even goes on the road for that, which he tells me is what happened this time. I really don't know all that much about what he does, but I know that for someone as young as he is he's doing really well. That's what my mother says when she's not putting him down, which is most of the time.

I remember this one time when I was little—this was when my parents were still together—and I got really curious about what my father did for a living and I started pestering my mother, what does Daddy do, what does Daddy do? I can't say why I didn't just ask him. They were always fighting. Maybe his yelling was louder and he scared me.

Mama didn't see why I shouldn't just ask him myself, which I finally did, but instead of telling me, he showed me. We went to the studio where he was working and he introduced me to all the people he worked with. One of the men there heard my voice and said I sounded really cute, and then my father said we should use my voice on a song they were working on. I forget what the name of the song is, but there's a CD out there with my voice on it right at the beginning, saying something—just baby talk, I guess. My mother used to have a copy but one time I was playing with it and it broke.

Daddy asks me how my summer is going, how my friends are doing, and if I'm taking care of Mama, which I'm happy to say I'm doing well. After he tells me he loves me and misses me and is looking forward to seeing me again it's time for him to go. "I love you, too, Daddy," I say, a little shaky, and hang up.

I walk back in the direction of the stairs hoping to make a clean break to my room, but my mother is sitting in the living room and calls me in to see her.

"Did you have a good talk with your father?" she asks.

I can tell she's still mad. "Yeah, it was fine," I say, hoping she won't ask me any more questions.

But she does. "Is he planning some kind of birthday celebration for you?"

"He says he wants to do something special with me the next time we're together, but he wouldn't tell me what it was."

She grunts. "Yeah, I'll bet he didn't. Probably wants to throw a lot of money at you, trying to impress you, trying to *spoil* you more like it. He knows how I feel about that. Sneaky little..." Mama takes a deep breath before continuing. "I don't know what I ever saw in that man that I could...forgetting your birthday. He's selfish, he's..."

She continues talking about him but she's not looking at me, and I start to wonder if she's even talking to me at all, if she still remembers I'm here. But I am here, listening to her talk about my father like she hates his guts.

"I'm going up to my room for a while, Mama," I say. Mother looks up, not talking now, just staring at me glassy-eyed.

"Okay, Baby Lark," she says, coming back to

earth. "Girl, why don't you get outside for a while? I'm telling you, it's a beautiful day."

♦

Sneaky.

That's the way my mother describes my father, but I'd say it's a pretty good way to describe her as well. It's a beautiful day, she says. Get out and enjoy yourself in that gorgeous sun, she says. I should have known she wanted something out of the deal but like an idiot I looked out the window and decided maybe she was right. Up to my room for a quick wardrobe change (underwear doesn't always go over big outside the house), out the door and into the backyard to say goodbye and, like the master she is, my mother casually ropes me into helping her out in her garden. Amazing. How does she do it? I didn't even see it coming.

Work.

Work on my vacation.

And not just any work. Physical work, lifting stuff and moving stuff and raking around in the dirt, in the *fertilizer*. I have no problem with getting into a mess, but it has to be for the right reasons. Goofing off with your friends is the right reason. Being chased by some boy through a muddy field and maybe even tripping and falling head first but dragging him down into the mud along with you is the right reason.

Helping your mother in her garden and having to lift stuff and move stuff is *not* the right reason.

Right now we're planting an apple tree—a second one because, Mama tells me, you need two apple trees so they can cross-pollinate. "It's the only way the apples will grow strong and healthy, Lark," Mama says.

Whatever.

Mama's telling me about when she was a kid in Guyana and how she lived at the edge of a field of apple trees. Her granny used to send her out to pick apples all the time, which she would use to make apple jam and apple sauce and apple butter. Saying how she's been wanting apple trees for years, reminds her of her grandmother, of home, and now she's finally got them. I giggle. I'm saying, it's only an apple tree, Mama. What's the big deal? Mama giggles back but I can tell she's serious when she says, "Hey, it was something I wanted. Having apple trees was a dream. Everybody's gotta have a dream, Lark."

Huh.

Now she's getting ready to start digging the hole to put the tree in. It's not far from the first tree, which I remember she put in just fine without my help. "Here, read this to me," she says, handing me a piece of paper with planting instructions. "I just need you to find me the part where it says how deep to dig the hole. I don't remember any more."

I flip through the paper. "It just says you have to dig it one and a half times the size of the pot the tree is in, and make the hole two feet wide."

Mama starts digging. Man, look at her go! She's so strong, but you'd never really think that to look at her. She's really tall and skinny and she's got what she calls "real child-bearing hips." My favorite are her dreadlocks, so long and beautiful, she looks like a queen when she walks all graceful like she does, her hair flowing down around her face.

But just look at her now—hair tied back, dirt all over her, taking on the earth and winning.

If she's this strong and can do all this stuff herself, what does she need me for?

"Guy, Lark, if it's such a chore for you to hang out here, don't let me keep you," she says.

Uh-oh. She sounds a little mad.

"I'm not mad, I'm just...I don't know, I don't

think it's a crime for a mother to want to spend a little time with her daughter. You stick your little face in front of that TV or go out gallivanting with your friends. I barely remember your face. In fact, I'm not even sure you're my daughter." Mama stops shoveling and leans in near my face like she needs a closer look, real serious looking. "Who are you, girl?"

"I'm Lark."

"*Lark?* Lark who?"

"Ha, ha," I say.

"Yeah, I suppose you are my daughter, aren't you. I'm sorry, Lark, I didn't recognize you," she says, starting to smile a little now.

Mama slowly starts digging again. "I mean, hey, I know what's it's like. I don't blame you if you want to run around with your friends. You're stuck in that classroom all those months. Come the summer you just want to get out there with your cronies and go wild, or you want to sit around, not have to think and catch up on a few of your favorite shows, just because you can. Am I right?"

I tell her she is.

"I understand that. I really do. I just want to

spend a little time with you while you're still young enough to enjoy hanging out with your mother. God knows my mother and I stopped enjoying each other's company soon enough. I remember one time, I was around fourteen or fifteen and I'd been seeing this boy for a while—a couple of months, I guess—and when I finally got around to bringing him home, my mother flipped. She's going, how could I go out with this low life, this guy was going to ruin my life, blah, blah, blah. I mean, I'm fourteen years old. I don't know what she was expecting, I wasn't gonna marry him or anything. I think the real reason she went so crazy was because I hadn't shown her the proper respect in bringing him around as soon as I met him for her to approve or disapprove of. Like I'm supposed to get her blessing. They're real big on respect for your elders in Guyana, especially when I was growing up."

"So what are you saying, Mama, that a kid *shouldn't* respect her elders?"

Mama looks at me, grinning.

I grin back.

Mama says, "I guess I walked into that one. No, smarty pants, I don't mean you shouldn't respect your elders. Of course you should. I just mean...I don't know, I'm just talking to you, I guess."

Mama stops talking for a minute, concentrating on her digging. Out of nowhere she says, "So tell me, Baby Lark, are there any boys out there you're interested in?"

"What?" I say. Uh-oh, she heard how I said that. Now she's going to ask me again, just watch, I know her.

"You heard me," she says. (Told you!) "Are there any kids out there you're interested in?" Look at the grin on her face. "If there're any boys you wanna bring 'round for me to meet, I'd love to meet 'em. You don't have to sneak around behind my back. I promise I'll be nice to your little boyfriend."

"Of course there aren't any boys." I take my glasses off and put them back on my face just to have something to do with my hands.

"Really? Pretty young girl like you? I find that hard to believe. What about some of those fellas at your birthday party? What about that kid, Robby—what was that nickname you guys had for him—Robby something..."

"Robby *Roastbeef*?!"

"Yeah, that was it!"

"*No way! Ooohh!* Talk about nasty, guy Mama, I don't put you down."

She's laughing by this point, but I can't see the joke, can you? She mumbles something about remembering what it was like, not liking boys as a kid, and then puts her arms around me and says, "Okay, okay, I'm sorry. I wasn't trying to put you down." I think this is finally the end but she keeps right on going, laughing still as she says, "What about that kid that showed up late with the skateboard..."

I have to stop her right there.

I put my hands up to her mouth and hold them there, 'cause there's no way I'm gonna hear the end of that sentence. First Argy and Jennifer, and now my own mother?

Mama's laughing. She takes my hands from her mouth and says, "Oh, but he was so sweet, him walking around so proud of that skateboard. I thought he was adorable."

Skip. He even got to my own mother...

And then she kills me with one simple line.

"And," she says, "I thought the two of you made such a cute couple."

4 | Lark and the Motorboy at War

Let the summer beware. I am Lark, hear me roar.

Up bright and early, a quickie breakfast, a quickie goodbye to my mother and I'm out. The summer sun is mine. Decided the time had come to take my mother's advice and get out and enjoy the summer while I have the chance.

I used to be blown away by all the different things you could do in the summer. It was like there was so much stuff to do and only two months to do it. It could drive you crazy trying to fit it all in, or just trying to decide what to do first. But after ten years of this I'm a summer veteran. I know just how to squeeze the most out of the day. There's no way I'm going back to school in September feeling like I let the months slip through my fingers.

I am Lark. Hear my roar.

This morning my roar sounds like a doorbell that won't stop. I'm leaning on Jennifer's doorbell.

Why won't someone come and open the door?

Finally I hear footsteps, loud, stomping. Someone's not happy. I'm beaming at Jennifer's mother as she opens the door.

"Hi, Mrs. Story!"

She can't be mad at me when I put on my little cutie face, smiling up at her like a lost puppy, big eyes. Looks like she just got out of bed. Her hair's plastered to the side of her head or sticking straight up like a fright wig. She's wiping the sleep from her eyes.

"Is Jennifer home?" I walk in.

"Come right in, Lark," Mrs. Story says. "I think Jennifer's still sleeping. Like *I* was trying to do."

"Can I go upstairs and get her?" I say, as I start running up the stairs.

I burst open the door to Jennifer's room. There's Sleeping Beauty curled up in bed.

"WAKE UP!" I yell.

Jennifer jumps out of bed and lands on the floor. I rush up and start shaking her. "What are you doing?" I say. "It's almost 9:30 and you're still sleeping. What's going on? Wake up!"

I'm still shaking her and she's saying, "I'm awake, I'm awake!"

"Boy, you and your mom," I say. "Why does everyone in this house sleep so late?"

"What are you talking about? You sleep late in the summer, too."

"Yeah, well, I'm awake now, and it's time for us to go."

"Go where? What are you doing here? What time did you say it was?"

Man, what a flake.

When I was walking up her driveway I heard this banging going on. It sounded like it was coming from the back of the house, so I say, "Do you know what that banging was all about?"

Jennifer perks up. "Oh, that's right," she says as she runs up to her bedroom window. When I go to see what she's looking at, I see her father up in one serious-looking treehouse.

"He said he was gonna finish it this morning, but I forgot." Jennifer's beaming now, she's so excited.

"*Wow*," I say.

Jennifer rushes around putting on her clothes and then she grabs my arm and pulls me out of the room, and the next thing I know we're in the back-yard, Jennifer hugging her father who's on the ground now, looking up and admiring what he's created.

"Hi, Mr. Story," I say. "Did you build that all yourself?"

"All myself," he says. "Been up since five this morning putting the finishing touches on it. Still have to do a few more things. I want to put some shelves in there eventually, and maybe some thick curtains over the windows for when it gets colder, but it's essentially done. What do you think, honey?"

"Oh, I just love it, Dad," Jennifer says. She's so thrilled she can't keep still, and I can't say I blame her. The treehouse is *amazing*. Large and really nicely built. It's placed between three trees they have that are growing close together like a little mini-forest, but also it rests on what look like four long legs. Mr. Story calls them pillars. There's a ladder built onto one of the trees and another one comes down from the center of the treehouse's floor. He's put windows on each side. There's even a front door and a little porch. I'm telling you, the thing is great.

I've been hearing about this treehouse for a couple of years now but this is the first time I've actually seen all of it. Practically every time I came by it was covered with a huge tarp so you could only see little chunks of it at a time. Jennifer's father is a carpenter. He promised to build the treehouse for her and her younger brother Jerry years ago but since he only got the chance to work on it on weekends and then only when the weather was nice, it took a long time. But it's a good thing he took his time with it. Ain't no regular cheesy little treehouse this.

"Looks like you could fit, like, six, seven people in there," I say.

"Oh, if they're all your size then, yeah, no problem," Mr. Story says. He turns to Jennifer, putting his arm around her. "No more than that, though, okay, honey? It's plenty safe, but it's better not to push these things. I'm going to tell your brother the same thing."

Jennifer promises up and down that she won't and thanks her father a million times. Mr. Story tells us if we want to go up and check the thing out go right ahead. "I turn the keys over to you, Ms. Story," he says, bowing, and me and Jennifer giggle and are up the ladder in a flash.

The treehouse is even more incredible inside.

Ton of space to move around, to lay out your sleeping bags, we don't have to crouch or anything. Even a couple of adults could hang out in here and not be too crowded. I look out and I can almost see for miles around. The view is awesome.

"The only sucky thing is you have to share it with your brother," I say.

"Well, Dad built it for the two of us. I love my brother. Why would it be a problem?"

Whatever.

Jennifer says, "I can't wait 'til Argy sees this place. She's gonna *freak*."

Don't I know it. "We should go get her now!"

"Now? I just got up, Lark. Let me at least put on my clothes first."

Twenty-three minutes later, after we've run down the block to get Argy and run back, the three of us are having breakfast in the treehouse, christening it.

I'm excited. My mind is racing, my mouth is racing. I'm making plans for the treehouse. Parties and sleepovers and bigger stuff—secret things I can't quite describe properly but I know we have to do.

Jennifer cuts me off. "Hey, what are you talking about, Lark? This is *my* treehouse."

"What do you mean?"

"I mean, you're making all these plans for the place. Dad built it for *me*. It's not yours."

"But we're a team. What are you saying? You're not even gonna share?"

"Of course I'm gonna share. I'm just saying..."

Argy says, "It's not like that, Lark."

"I think it *is* like that," I say. "Don't be so greedy, Jennifer."

"I'm not being greedy. It's *my* treehouse. *I'm* the one who gets to decide what happens in it."

"It's not just your treehouse. Jerry gets some say, too."

"I know he does!"

"And as your friends, I think it's only right we get some say as well."

Jennifer grunts. I go on. "'Cause I can see really big things happening in here."

"Like what?" Jennifer says.

"I don't know...*yet*," I say.

I'm thinking, just change the subject, Lark.

So I say, "So what are we doing today, Divas? We got the whole summer. Let's not waste it."

"Swimming?"

"Barbies?"

"Bike riding?"

"Sailor Moon!"

That's the one.

"I get to be Sailor Moon," I yell. "Called it."

Jennifer starts whining. "Ahh, you *always* get to be Sailor Moon."

"That's 'cause I always call it."

Jennifer starts going on and on about wanting to be Sailor Moon, but what does she want me to do? I already called it. It's not my fault she's not fast enough.

Argy says, "Actually, I don't want to be Sailor Moon. I prefer to be Sailor Venus." Atta girl.

Jennifer says, "All right, fine. I'll be Sailor *Mars*– the one that thinks Sailor Moon is a brat. But next time, no matter what, I'm being Sailor Moon."

"We'll see," I say. Yeah. Like there's any chance of that.

◆

"MOON TIARA MAGIC!" I yell. I may not have a real tiara but I've got my Sailor Moon super model pose down.

Demons from the Negaverse attack us in front of Jennifer's house. I want to stay and fight but wimpy Sailor Venus doesn't think we can handle it without the help of Tuxedo Mask. I argue but suddenly the demons get to Sailor Venus and stun her. Knowing it's up to me and Sailor Mars, we turn a couple of demons into bubbles and then grab the wounded Sailor Venus. We'll take the demons on again later, but for right now we have to escape! We can't go back to the treehouse. The Negaverse demons might have taken it over. Right now they could be crawling inside it, trying to discover our secrets. So we decide our only choice is to run deep into the forest.

The forest is near our houses. I want to run straight through to the other side so we can hang out at the pond and watch the ducks and their little duck families swimming around but Jennifer has a different idea.

I yell, *"Wait,"* but it's too late. Her and Argy are running down a path so I follow. Ten feet ahead of me, Jennifer's foot gets caught in a root and she goes flying. Argy's right behind her and trips over Jennifer sprawled out on the ground. I run up and drop to my knees beside them. I'm laughing so hard my stomach's hurting.

I say, "I told you we should've kept on running but, no, you always gotta do things your way. You never want to listen to Lark. Now look at the two of you."

Argy says she just didn't hear me. Jennifer tells me to shut up. She says, "Why should we always do everything your way? What makes your way always so special?"

I'm about to say that with my way you don't wind up tripping over roots, but Jennifer cuts me off by jumping on me, and suddenly the three of us are rolling around on the ground giggling, a Sailor Scout fight to the finish.

I win of course. I always win. I am Lark. Hear me roar.

We lie on our backs and look up at the clouds passing over the trees. I pretend the trees are the legs of giants so tall their bodies are covered up by the clouds.

Argy's in the middle of a story about this time when she went swimming with this stuck-up girl from school when she looks over and sees a snake slithering through the leaves. She screams and jumps up and starts running. She's yelling, *"SNAKE! SNAKE!"* and as soon as we hear that we're up in a shot following her, 'cause Sailor Scouts or not, we ain't taking on no snakes.

We make our way to the other side of the woods.

I say, "Hey, did you two hear that?"

"Hear what?" Jennifer says.

"I thought I heard voices. Like, *boys'* voices..."

I get back into Sailor Moon mode. I tell the girls to get behind me and we crouch quietly along the path, cutting through trees and dense bush until we come out of the woods and see a bunch of guys hanging around the duck pond. There's about six of them and they've all got toy guns and toy rifles. One of them has a skateboard with him.

Argy says, "Is that the Motorboy down there?"

Jennifer says, "Oh, that's him all right," and then she turns and looks at me, big stupid grin on her face which I decide not to slap off.

They're playing their dumb war games. Look at them shooting each other, falling down, getting back up. Why do all their games have to be so stupid? Why do they have to die and be so violent all the time? Tanya's stinky little brother Sheldon is down there. I see him grab something from the ground and take off with it. In a flash Skip is on his skateboard after him, shooting him with his gun, but he finally has to come off the thing and chase Sheldon on foot 'cause the skateboard won't work on the grass properly. He catches up to the guy and tackles him to the ground. He shoots Sheldon again and grabs whatever it is he took, jumping up laughing and running back to the other guys.

Looking at Skip, I remember the last time I saw him with his pants around his knees, and wonder if he's thought about trying the same trick on me. Maybe if he knew I was crouching here spying on him he'd get his boys together and try to corner me and, man, then he'd see a war.

Jennifer and Argy start giggling. Argy says, "Let's go over and talk to them."

I say, "What for?"

Jennifer says, "Aw, she just wants to 'cause Robby Roastbeef's down there."

"I do not!" Argy says.

"You do so."

I surprise myself by getting up and walking out of the woods toward the boys, forgetting about Skip probably wanting revenge. I can hear Jennifer and Argy behind me, suddenly getting scared, not so mouthy now they might actually have to go talk to the boys. Finally they come out and join me, and the three of us, the Sailor Scouts together again, walk up to the boys and stand there in front of them, challenging them to say something.

I cross my arms and raise my head, thinking, just try me.

I lock eyes with Skip the Motorboy. We size each other up.

Skip crosses his arms and steps toward me.

We all stand there staring. No one says a word.

Finally, "Who're you three supposed to be, the Pansy Brigade?" Skip says. A couple of the guys laugh. Ooh, Skip, you're such a tough guy.

I say, "Who're you guys supposed to be, the *Idiot* Brigade?" Good one. The girls laugh. A couple of the guys react. "I see you're wearing your belt pretty tight there, Skip. What's the matter, afraid someone's gonna come along and pull your pants down?" Now the girls really bust up, but the guys stand there looking at each other, confused. Ooh, big surprise, Skip decided to keep his mouth shut about our little adventure.

Skip says, "What do you want, *four-eyes?*" sounding mad.

"Who says we want something, *Dumbo?* Why don't you flap your ears and fly away?" Even a couple of the boys try and hold in laughs over that one.

"What, you got a problem with us hanging around here?"

"Did I say I had a problem?"

"Well, what do you want, Lark?"

"I'm not Lark, I'm Sailor Moon. This is Sailor Venus and this is Sailor Mars. We're the Sailor Scouts."

Some of the guys start laughing, but Skip doesn't, he just stands there, eyes still locked to mine. He says, "Let me ask you a question. How come Sailor Moon is the leader, huh? I mean, she's just a moon. The other girls are whole planets, but they gotta take orders from some moon?"

I have to say I've wondered about that, too, but I'm not about to admit it to him. I say, "'Cause that's the way it is, *Skip*. Nice name by the way."

"Oh, yeah? Well, it's better 'n being named after a bird."

Ooh...good one.

Skip says, "You know what I say? I say your little Sailor Brigade is *nothing*, so why don't you take your little rusty behinds and get on out of here."

"Why don't you and your little band of losers make us?"

"There's six of us and there's only three of you. And...you're only *girls.*"

The guys start cackling again, high-fivin' Skip and I suddenly yell, *"Shut up!"* real loud, and they all just freeze and look at me. Jennifer and Argy are speechless but Skip is sort of grinning. Then everyone starts laughing.

I say, "We'll take you six stink boys on any day of the week."

I challenge them to a duel right then and there. Some of the guys look uncomfortable. I'm hearing things like, "I don't want to play with them," like, "You can't play with *girls,*" like, "I'm going home," but Skip just says, "You're not going anywhere. What are you, afraid of a girl? There's six of us, there's three of them. If they think they can take us on, let 'em. It'll be their funeral."

Some of the guys here were at my party the other day. There's stinky Sheldon and his pal Raymond, there's Robby Roastbeef, Skip, of course, and a couple of guys I've never seen before. Robby Roastbeef keeps looking up and catching Argy looking at him and then they both look away. All these boys seem pretty shifty-eyed. If it's a fight they want that's what they're going to get. I lock eyes with Skip again. I can tell he feels the same way.

He invites me aside for a war council. My girls look a little scared to be left alone but I tell them to be strong. I remind them they are *women* and that these *boys* cannot touch them. Then the war council begins.

"I'm a nice guy," Skip says. "Which is why I'll let you choose the game."

I say, "No, no, no. I want *you* to choose. I don't want to hear how we chose a wuss game 'cause we're girls. I want to beat you at your game played your way."

Skip smiles. He runs his fingers along his skateboard. In my mind I laugh at the guy, him trying to convince me the stupid thing's a motorcycle. He says, "All right. Capture the Flag. I'm sure you understand the rules. We have a flag, you have a flag. We hide our flag, you hide yours. Either team gets caught in the other team's zone trying to find their flag, they go to jail—"

"Yeah, I know how to play the game."

"Okay, but you know there are more of us than

there are of you. What happens if all of your guys, sorry, *girls*, get caught? I'll tell you what, you're out of the game. You want some of my men to even things out?" Skip grins.

And I laugh right in his face. "Yeah, right. You think I want any of them nasties playing on my side? I'd rather take all of you on by *myself* than even things out that way. In five minutes they'd try and take over or try and mess us up so your side could win, or something. Besides, that goes both ways. You could capture all of us, but we could capture all of you. You know why? 'Cause anything *boys* can do, *girls* can do better."

Skip smiles again. "Like I said, it's your funeral."

We walk back to our teams. Argy is trying to take Robby Roastbeef's baseball cap away from him. He keeps putting his hands on his head to stop her and running away but then he giggles and lets her get near him again.

I gather my team and we huddle as I tell them what we're doing.

"Remember, girls, don't be afraid of them. They're just boys, they're nothing. We're women, we're Amazons, we're the Sailor Scouts. Nothing can touch us. Okay?"

They nod.

I stand and call over to Skip and his boys.

"We're ready."

And the war begins.

◆

I say to Skip, "I was surprised when you said that thing about Sailor Moon, about why she was the leader and not one of the planet Sailors. I actually wondered that, too. I never would've thought, like, a boy would be into that show."

Me and Skip are walking around the sports field at our school. Before the game of Capture the Flag was even halfway finished, one of those guys I didn't recognize said he had to go. First I thought he was just upset 'cause even though we were losing we were doing better than he expected, but the *other* guy I didn't recognize turned out to be his brother and he also had to go. Next thing you know Argy's parents pulled up in their car. Now she's gotta go, too. Her parents had been driving around looking for her. She was supposed to have been home a while ago so they could all go out.

After that, the game just kind of fell apart. Everybody sort of drifted away. Pretty soon it's just me and Skip and Jennifer standing around looking at each other. Then Jennifer said *she* wanted to go.

I said, "C'mon, stick around a while. It's still early."

I kinda got the impression Skip was making her shy or something, I don't know. I'm thinking, what do you have to be shy about? What's he gonna do, bite?

Even Skip tried to get her to stay. "It's too early to go home. The summer's gonna be over before you know it. You go home now it's like going home on a weekend to do homework," Skip said, and I agreed with him. I think even Jennifer felt that way but she still said she had to go so me and her walked off.

We were near her place when I said I'd see her later. She invited me in but I said I wanted to get home, too, so I said bye and walked off in the direction of my house. But I didn't go home. I waited until Jennifer went back inside and then I snuck back to where we were hanging out with the Motorboy. I ran into him walking through the woods. Here's Skip acting all stuck up, saying, What, did you forget something? And I'm going, No, regretting going back there.

So here I am now with Skip just walking

around. He keeps hopping on his skateboard, sliding for a while, jumping off and walking beside me. He keeps asking me if I want a ride but I always say, "No, I don't want a ride, big head. I already told you that. Why you keep asking me?" He just laughs and hops back on his board.

I cannot believe I'm hanging out with this guy. I keep thinking, what if someone I know sees the two of us together? What am I going to do then?

I say, "We would have kicked your ass at Capture the Flag, you know. If we'd got the chance to finish the game."

Skip snorts. "Yeah, *right*. I told the guys to ease off. I felt sorry for you 'cause it was just the three of you girls."

"You were not, Skip. You guys were sweating. You couldn't even keep up."

Skip laughs. "You know, Lark, that was pretty rough what you pulled on me the other day, pulling my pants down in front of those girls." I start laughing. "I mean, what was that all about? I was just offering you a ride on my board."

"Yeah, well, that was pretty rough what you pulled on me, showing up at my birthday party. I look up and suddenly your ugly face is standing there."

"Well, your mama didn't seem to have too much of a problem with me showing up. And if I'm so ugly, why're you hanging out with me, huh?"

I feel my face get warm. "'Cause I don't have nothing better to do."

We walk to the end of the field, through the dense, thick bushes and down the hill into the creek at the bottom. We practice jumping from one side to the other. I have to go up the hill a bit and run down fast to jump to the other side. Skip's way taller than me so he doesn't have to run up at all. He just has to step back a bit. I watch him jump over the creek in one go and I forget myself for a second and say, "Wow." I regret it immediately. Skip looks at me, kind of surprised. He tries to jump to the other side again but instead of at least stepping back he gets all cocky and tries to clear it from where he's standing, and he winds up missing the opposite edge by about a half foot. A loud splash, water spraying. Now he's lying on the other side of the creek with his leg in the water.

I start laughing, and I'm a little surprised when

Skip starts laughing, too. I'm sort of happy he's laughing. He stands up and says, "Did you see that? I was like Superman except for at the end there."

"You were like Superman except you forgot how to fly. You should have flapped your ears."

We keep laughing about it. We walk up and down the creek skipping rocks and looking for frogs. At this shallow part of the creek, Skip tries to ride his skateboard in the water and he actually gets it to work. He asks me if I want a ride in the water but I say what I always say—no.

Later when the sun's starting to go down, we're walking around and we find this big paper bag filled with money-back bottles of Tahiti Treat and Pepsi and stuff. We both freak out. There's gotta be seven or eight dollars' worth of bottles in there, so before anyone can see us, we grab the bag and run to the Mac's Milk nearby.

Twenty minutes later we're sitting in a park on the swings with two big bags full of goodies in front of us.

In between munching a Crunchie I say to Skip, "I gotta start thinking 'bout getting home."

Skip pops a jaw breaker into his mouth. Like an

idiot he tries to bite down on it and almost breaks his teeth. I say, "What are you doing, stupid head? Haven't you ever had a jaw breaker before? What a guy."

Skip shrugs, taking the candy out of his mouth and looking at it. He holds it, licking it slowly and says, "Hey, before you go home, you want to have a ride on my motorcycle?"

"No, I don't. Why you keep asking me that? All day long you been asking me. And that's something else. Why do you keep calling the thing a motorcycle? Ain't no motorcycle, it's a skateboard."

I pick the board up and hold it in front of his face so he can see the picture of the turtle on the bottom. "Does this look like a motorcycle to you?"

Skip chuckles. "Okay, okay. Would you like to have a ride on my *skateboard*."

"No, I would not."

"You sure? I'll even let you ride on it by yourself."

"Naw. I don't really even know how to ride one properly."

"I'll teach you."

"No."

"All right."

He sounded kind of sad when I said that. I didn't

really want to hurt his feelings so I say, "Maybe I'll try it another time."

I look over at the Motorboy and it occurs to me that we've pretty much spent the day together. I start to wonder what he'll be doing after I leave, which'll be pretty soon. My mother's probably wondering where I am by now.

I say, "You know, you're sure a lot different from the way you act at school and around your friends."

Skip says, "It's funny. I was thinking the same thing about you. You're a lot nicer by yourself."

"I gotta get going, Skip."

"All right, cool. Can I walk home with you?"

"Yeah, but if you think you're coming in, you're out of your mind."

◆

I eat dinner with Mama and then later after I finish washing the dishes I settle down to watch some TV. Mama comes and sits down in front of the television, spends a couple of minutes doing the parent thing, saying, "Lark, why do you have to watch so much TV? Go read a book or something," before falling asleep on the couch. When I hear her snoring, I'm a little irritated because I can't listen to my show properly, but I'm also happy 'cause I'd rather listen to her snoring than her complaining.

The phone rings. I look over at Mama, hoping she'll get up because I'm at a good part in my show, but coma woman ain't budging. I groan real loud and force myself out of the La-Z-Boy.

"Hello?" I say, as polite as I can force myself. My mother doesn't like it when I answer the phone the way I usually do. She always says I sound...*surly*, I think she calls it.

It's some man on the phone, deep, deep voice, a lot like my father's. He says his name is Milton and that I must be Lark, he's heard so much about me from my mother. He says what a sweet-sounding little girl I am and I'm thinking, Save it for the next chump, buddy, 'cause I'm not buying, but I just say thank you. He makes cute talk for a couple of minutes, asking me how old I am and what grade I'm in, blah, blah, blah, and then, *finally*, he asks me if my mother's in and can he speak to her.

I say, "She's sleeping right now. Can I take a message?"

"Lark, honey, it's a matter of some importance. I'd really appreciate it if you'd go and wake your mother for me."

I don't like that. I don't like people calling me stuff like honey when they don't even know me.

I tell Milton again that Mama's sleeping but he won't give up so I finally say, "Okay, hold on a minute," not sounding so lady-like this time.

I wake Mama up. She asks who it is and when I say, "Some guy named Milton," she grins and groans at the same time. I tell her I tried to tell him that she was sleeping but he wouldn't take no for an answer.

She says it's okay and walks over to the phone, wiping the sleep from her eyes.

I try to go back to watching my TV show but I'm finding I'm more interested in my mother's phone conversation. I sit up in my chair and look in the direction of the kitchen, trying to listen. Mama laughing a little but sounding sort of impatient, talking to him like she really wants to get off the phone. She keeps saying stuff like, "I can't talk right now," and "Why are you calling so late," and "I'll talk to you later." Just the same it takes her forever to get off the phone.

When I hear her hang up, I sit back down in the chair quick and make myself look as comfortable as possible so Mama won't know I've been spying.

I even close my eyes a little so I look kind of bored and tired.

Mama sits down. I say, "You missed the good part. Captain Janeway almost had to blow up Voyager." Mama doesn't look all that interested.

"Was that one of your friends?" I ask, real casual.

After a second Mama says, "Naw. That was some guy from work. He's been asking me out. I told him no, but he keeps asking."

"How come he keeps asking you out?"

"I guess because he likes me, Lark."

"Does Daddy know about this?"

Mama looks at me funny. "Why would your father know anything about this? What, you want me to clear it with him?"

"No, I just—"

"Who I choose to go or not go out with is none of your father's business, Lark."

"Are...are you going to go out with this man?"

"I'm not planning on it. He is nice, but..."

I'm relieved, that's all I want to hear, but she keeps going.

"I already told him no. I sorta resent the fact that he keeps pushing me, you know? If I told him no once, shouldn't that be good enough?"

Just like Skip and his stupid skateboard—always asking me if I want a ride on the thing. I already told him no once...

I go over and rest my head on my mother's shoulder. "I know what you mean, Mama," I say. "Men are nothing but trouble."

5 | Fun with Mama and Daddy

The doorbell rings and I jump up and run for the door, but just before I reach it I see Mama's face, all sour looking, and I immediately try not to look so excited.

Forget it. I throw the door open and there he is standing there, smiling. I almost scream, *"Hi, Daddy,"* and I jump in his arms and practically knock him over and we're standing in the doorway beaming at each other.

"Hey, gorgeous, how you been? I missed you."

I say, "I missed you, too, Daddy," and then he's snarfing me and growling at me like a lion and I'm laughing.

Daddy walks in, and seeing Mama looking at us, he puts me down and says, "Hey, Dexter."

"Hello, Arthur. How are you?"

"I'm good."

They look at each other for a moment. I'm so happy to have the three of us together, I'm there with this huge grin on my face.

Daddy looks down at me standing by his legs, his hands on my shoulders, and says, "So, hey, kid. We're gonna have a good time the next few days. I'm sorry I couldn't get to you on your birthday, but you look like you survived okay."

Mama snorts.

Daddy says, "If you have something to say, Dexter, say it."

But Mama doesn't say anything else to Daddy. She kneels down beside me and says, "Now, baby, I want you to have a great time with your father, okay? Mama loves you. I'm going to miss you a lot."

I tell her I'm going to miss her as well. As I'm walking out of the house, I hear Mama say to Daddy, "I know you're gonna take good care of my daughter, Arthur."

Then I hear Daddy say, "She's my daughter, too."

◆

Late at night, I'm lying in bed thinking about the wonderful time I've spent with my father. He's such a great guy. The whole drive over from my house to his house he told me over and over he was sorry he missed my birthday and that he was determined to make it up to me, and I kept saying, It's okay. I know you had to work. But it still seemed to bother him.

Our first day together Daddy dropped his "big surprise" on me which turned out to be lunch at McDonald's. I didn't have the heart to tell him that Mama takes me to McDonald's all the time. That night we went to dinner at a fancier place. I drank Shirley Temples 'til I felt like I was gonna float away, and then Daddy got this woman with a huge chest to sing me Happy Birthday. The best part, Daddy didn't make me finish my vegetables the way Mama does.

What a guy.

The second day we went swimming at this pool near his house and later we played Chinese Checkers and I beat him three times. In the afternoon he took me to the music studio he's working at to pick up some stuff he wanted to work on at home.

Today Daddy had some work he wanted to finish so I mostly hung around by myself. I slept in and then watched TV for a while. When that got boring I decided to go outside. At first I was just playing in my father's backyard. I looked in the bushes for bugs and then I played on the swings he set up for me but that got old fast, so I decided to check out the neighborhood.

That was boring, too. Nothing but a bunch of adults walking around, old men with canes and stuff. I started thinking about the Motorboy, wondering what he was doing. He's been on my mind a lot lately and it's been bothering me. The first night I was at my father's I even had a dream about him and I was so embarrassed I tried to make myself forget it immediately. But I guess I still remember.

I'd been wandering around for about an hour when I saw a group of kids hanging around the playground of this building. There was a big circle of kids my age so I went up to see what was going on. As I got closer I could hear all this yelling and stuff. Sure enough, there was a fight going on. Turns out some guy mouthed off to another guy in front of his friends and you know how boys are. No one wanted to back down so there they were going at it. So stupid! Why do boys have to go on like that? Instead of talking to each other they gotta hit each other to make a point, *oooohh*, they're *so* coo—

"*HEY, YOU KIDS!*"

Boom, everyone scattered. I didn't know what was going on so I stood there a second. Then I saw this old man rushing up to us carrying a cane, walking so fast he had to hold on to his hat so it didn't fly off. The old man was a monster, a demon, a Negaverse demon. I saw horns coming from his head. I saw his eyes turn red and start to shine. I saw fire in his mouth and nostrils. I saw his hands turn to claws and I forgot I was Sailor Moon and I ran, I ran for my life.

He was yelling, "What the hell do you kids think you're doing," stuff like that, but I didn't hear the rest. I was too far away. I didn't know where I was going, but suddenly this girl I'd seen earlier called out to me and I ran up to her. She was behind a wood plank wall at the end of the playground, hiding in the bushes behind it. There was some other kid with her, some guy, both of them crouched behind there, shivering and giggling.

I said, "What was that all about?"

The girl said, "That's Mr. Winter. He lives in the building. I think he hates kids or something. We're just hanging around or whatever and he stands on his balcony yelling at us. Sometimes he comes down and tries to chase us off, like just now."

I started laughing. Every time I get scared and then it's over, I start laughing. I don't know why. The girl and the guy started laughing, too. The girl asked me where I was from. I said I lived downtown and was just visiting my father for a few days. The girl asked if my parents were divorced or something and I said no, they just didn't live together any more.

The girl said the guy with us in the bushes was her little brother. She said that their parents were divorced. She said that they lived with their father and that he hated their mother's guts, said bad stuff about her all the time. She said that they wished they lived with their mother because their father didn't really love them.

I said, "Well, my father loves me a lot."

The girl said, "You're lucky."

Later me and Daddy went for a drive. We drove by the lake and watched the boats sail around the harbor. We drove around the city and looked at the lights from the buildings and later, after we'd gotten Taco Bell from a drive-thru window, we drove to the airport and watched planes land and take off.

When we got home Daddy told me it was time for bed and he tucked me in and started reading *Green Eggs and Ham* but I wasn't really listening and finally he asked me what I was thinking.

We started talking about him and Mama. I asked if they were getting a divorce.

"Lark, you know your mother and I are divorcing."

I asked him why.

"Well, honey, that's a complicated question. Sometimes people drift apart. It just happens. It's nobody's fault."

He was silent for a little while but I asked him to keep talking.

"This is really important to you to talk about, huh?"

I said it was.

Daddy stroked my hair. He said, "Well, I can understand that. You and I haven't really spoken much about this. Your mother's a wonderful woman, Lark, but I think she's also a little immature in a lot of ways. There were times when I felt as though I was dealing with a daughter more than a wife. Do you understand what I'm talking about, Lark?"

I nodded but I really didn't. What did he mean immature? Mama doesn't act like a kid. She takes care of me. I'm the kid.

"Anyway, it doesn't matter," Daddy said. "I'm sure your mother has problems with me, too."

"Daddy, do you still love Mama?"

Daddy took a long time to answer me. He made a whole bunch of faces and sighed real heavy. "Well...you know, Lark...I still care about what happens to her...and I wish there was some way we could still be friends, but I don't think your mother wants that. And, frankly, *I'm* not sure it would be a good thing, either. I'll always want the best for her, and I'll always be connected to her through you. Nothing can change that."

I lied. I said, "Mama talks about you all the time, Daddy. She always says to me that she wishes you and her could still be together."

Daddy looked at me funny, almost shaking his head. He smiled and said, "Lark, baby, I think it's time you got some sleep."

And I've been trying to fall asleep since then but I can't. My mind keeps racing. I just don't understand. Every time Mama starts talking about Daddy all she does is put him down, but he never puts her down. She calls him a monster but I don't see him as a monster. He's a great guy. I love my father.

Maybe she knows something I don't. Maybe she knows him better than I do. Maybe he is a monster and I just don't see it for some reason. Maybe he's just making me *think* he's so great.

But, no, I...

And I start wondering, again, if it's my fault they're not together any more.

◆

Mama's waiting for us on the front steps of the house when Daddy and I pull in the driveway. She's drinking a Pepsi and reading a book. She walks over to the car as I hop out and give her a big hug.

"Hey, kid," she says. "You're doing pretty good I see." She turns to Daddy. "Hey, Arthur." Daddy says hey back. Mama surprises me a little when she says, "You want to come in for a drink? I could fix you something to eat if you're hungry."

Daddy accepts. He looks a little surprised himself.

We sit down in the kitchen, the three of us. We're a family again. Daddy takes the seat he always sat in when he lived here. As Mama pours him a tall glass of iced tea and sits down I beam, gazing back and forth at the two of them, my parents.

I'm telling Mama about my time with Daddy, really excited. Mama acts all excited, too, asking me questions, laughing with me. But she never looks in Daddy's direction. One time I'm talking about him for a long time and she just stares at the table.

I finish my drink and Mama tells me to go upstairs for a bath. I say it's way too early, I don't want to, but she gives me that look so I do as I'm told.

I hug Daddy hard.

He says, "All right, baby. You take care of yourself. I'll see you again real soon."

I walk upstairs to my room, change and then head down the hall to the bathroom, but I'm stopped by the sound of my parents. They're arguing. They sound mad but like they're trying to keep their voices low, I guess so I won't hear them. But here I am listening.

Or trying to. Mostly their voices are muffled. I hear my name a couple times, and Mama calling

Daddy bad names. Then Daddy *explodes*, his voice gets real clear, but I'm not listening any more.

I go to the bathroom and shut the door. I turn the water on full and when the bath is ready I get in and I stay in for a really long time.

6 Flying and Other Cool Stuff

It's later on the same day and I'm sitting on a curb, waiting.

After I got out of the bath I got dressed and cautiously went downstairs. I found Mama in the basement playing these old girl band records–The Ronettes, The Crystals. She loves that stuff. She was just lying on the floor on her back, a glass beside her, an arm over her eyes.

I walked up to her real quiet and whispered in her ear, "Mama." She took her arm from her eyes and looked at me. She took a sip of her drink. At first I thought it was pop but I got a whiff of it and it smelled *really* strong.

She looked sad.

I asked her if I could go out for a while.

She said, "Just make sure you're back before it gets dark."

I went out and headed in the direction of Jennifer's house, but I stopped and turned around. Instead I went a couple streets over and rang another doorbell.

Now Skip the Motorboy sits down on the curb beside me, resting his feet on his skateboard. He says, "Hey, sorry I kept you waiting."

"That's okay."

"You coulda waited inside while I got ready. My mom wouldn't mind. She likes to meet my friends."

At the sound of Skip calling me his friend I stand up and start down the sidewalk. Skip hops on that stupid skateboard and catches up, gliding along beside me.

"I can't stay out too long," I say.

"Hey, that's cool, neither can I. Actually, my moms wants me in the bath pretty soon. I'm surprised she let me out at all. And I'm really surprised you came to see me. Why'd you come by?"

"I don't know." I'm wondering myself why I went to see him. I don't even like the guy.

Skip's talking now, telling me he's glad I came. At least one of us is.

I say, "Are your parents still together?"

Surprised, Skip says, "Yeah. Why you ask that?"

"'Cause my parents don't live together any more. I was just wondering if yours did."

"Yeah. My mom says if my father even *looks* at another woman she's gonna skin him."

"Do you have any brothers or sisters or any-thing?"

"Well, mostly it's me, really. I got an older brother but he's all grown up, lives in L.A. now. But my moms is pregnant again, so I'm gonna have another brother or sister soon. I'm hoping for a sister to tell you the truth."

I'm surprised to hear this for some reason. I ask why he wants a sister and not a brother.

"I don't know...I just like the idea of having a younger sister, someone to take care of and stuff."

"You just want to push her around," I say.

"Hey, if it's a boy I could push him around just as easy. I'll be way older than him. Whatever, brother or sister, I don't really care. I'm just excit-ed. I can't wait. It's like, I miss my brother. My brother is the coolest guy, like, on the face of the earth. Nobody messes with him. If it came down to, like, Wolverine and my brother in a room or something, I'd pick my brother to win any day."

"How come your brother moved?"

"I don't know. For a long time I thought maybe it was something *I* did, like maybe he was moving to get away from me or something, 'cause I used to love hanging around him, and this one time he just, like, blew up at me. He's yelling, Stop bugging me all the time. And then about maybe six months later he moved out, and for a long time I thought he moved 'cause he hated me or something. But this other time he came back for a visit and he told me his moving out of the house didn't have nothing to do with me, so I guess I believe him..."

I kind of know what Skip's talking about. Sometimes I feel like that with my father, with his moving out, but I don't say that to Skip. I don't really say much of anything. I just listen to him. He tells me more about his family, about how his father works construction and about his mom who's a housewife and into soap operas or something, Skip's not really sure.

I watch Skip gliding on his skateboard, so graceful, the Silver Surfer, and I ask him, "Why do you always say that dumb thing is a motorcycle?"

He says he knows it's not really a motorcycle, *obviously* it's not. He says he's just pretending, what's wrong with that? I admit to myself that I really can't think of a reason why he shouldn't pretend it's a motorcycle if he wants to.

We come to the top of a hill, the sidewalk leading down into nothingness, and Skip the Motorboy hops on his skateboard/motorcycle, looking down at the hill, revving his engines, teetering on the edge, laughing. He pops the clutch and *flies* down the hill, and when he reaches the bottom he throws up his hands in victory, laughing even harder.

I run down the hill to meet him. My heart's pounding. I'm laughing, too. I say, *"Wow."* I'm saying that looked like serious fun. I'm thinking that looked *amazing. You* were amazing.

I ask him, "Can you teach me how to do that?"

"Man, I thought you'd never ask."

I want to start on the top of the hill but Skip says that would be a bad move. He says you can't just go down a hill like that your first time on a board. You go down a hill without knowing what you're doing, you're liable to break your neck. I'm sure he's right but I'm not listening. He looked so cool going down that hill. I want to do it, too. It's all I can think about. I keep bugging him and finally he says, okay, okay, it's your funeral, and we trudge up to the top of the hill.

Skip gives me a few pointers. Crouch low, keep your weight centered and steady, hold your arms out as support, blah, blah, blah.

"Can we just do this?"

"It's your funeral."

Skip puts his arms around me to steady me on the skateboard and I feel a little shiver go through my body. I want to giggle but instead I say, "Okay, stop touching me. Let's just do this."

Skip lets go of my waist

And I start down the hill

And I'm doing it, I'm really doing it, I'm

Flying, I'm

Flying down the hill, I'm

A goddess, I'm

Flying

And at the bottom of the hill I suddenly realize Skip hasn't taught me how to stop the skateboard. Either that or I wasn't listening, and now there's no way to stop the damn thing and I'm heading straight for a tree, so I dive off to the side and skid and roll on the ground—sky, ground, sky, ground, sky, ground...

Skip runs up to me, calling my name, looking worried. I sit up dusting myself off, laughing. Man, what a rush.

Skip starts laughing, too, and hands me my glasses which have fallen off in the crash. He says,

"Lark, you were great, girl," but I don't need him to tell me that.

I want more. But this time Skip convinces me to start learning with the easy stuff, so we go on flat ground. Skip puts his hands around my waist, and I forget that I don't want anyone to see me with him, and he guides me along on the skateboard, and I start to get the hang of it, and we're giggling together, and I start to like the way his hands feel on my waist, and somewhere in my brain I think that he's *nothing* like I thought he was.

◆

Later me and Skip sit on a curb. It's getting dark and we're not saying much, just looking around, and I know that I should be going but I'm sort of comfortable just sitting here with him.

His knee keeps brushing mine, and I'm really aware of it but I don't take my leg away. It sounds like he's about to say something so I say, "What?" But he says, no, he hasn't said anything.

I wonder what would happen if someone I knew saw the two of us sitting like this. I start thinking about that and then I realize I'm sitting on a curb with Skip the *stink* Motorboy...

"It's getting dark," I say. "I gotta go."

But I'm still sitting on the curb next to him.

Skip says, "Yeah, I should go, too. I promised my moms I was only gonna be gone for a little while."

But he's still sitting on the curb next to me.

Skip says, "I'll walk home with you."

"No, you gotta go. Your mom's gonna give you the beats."

His shoulder brushes against mine.

For some reason I say, "Have you ever kissed someone before?"

"What, you mean like a girl or something?"

"Yeah, stupid, I mean like a girl or something. And I don't mean your mom."

"I don't know...have you? Like...ever kissed a boy?"

"No."

"Why did you ask me that?"

"I just asked. God, don't make a big deal out of it."

We don't talk for a minute.

"So, have you?"

"Have I what?"

"Have you ever kissed a *girl*, dummy."

"Have you?"

"I already answered, stupid head. So, have you?"

"No."

We don't talk again. Then, for some reason I say, before I even know what words are going to come out of my mouth, "I want you to kiss me."

Skip looks at me funny, like he can't believe what I just said, and I know how he feels, but here I am looking into his eyes deep.

I lean closer to him.

I say, "I want you to kiss me on the lips..."

When I see Skip slowly leaning closer to me I close my eyes and I pucker my lips...

And I feel his lips against mine, pressing lightly...

And after a full minute of this I realize what I'm doing and I open my eyes and I see Skip already has his open, looking at me, and I pull my lips away and stand up suddenly, my hand against my mouth, not quite wiping it away.

I say, "I gotta go," and I start walking in the direction of my house, and I hear Skip behind me going, "Hey, Lark," but now I'm too far away. I can't hear him any more, and anyway I gotta get home before Mama tans my hide.

7 | I'll Bet TV People Never Have Days Like This

Tom is chasing Jerry around the room and is an inch away from grabbing his ta—*OH!* There's Jerry suddenly zipping to the right. He's burning toward a hole in the wall. Tom's on him now. Is he gonna grab him? He's almost got him, but no, Jerry zooms into his mousehole, and look, Tom can't stop in time. He's crashing into the wall!

I'm laughing my head off. Tom and Jerry, this show kills me. If only life were like that. On TV you smash your head right into a wall and get back up again.

Curled up on the La-Z-Boy watching TV, I'm not even out of my pajamas yet. The phone rings. Perfect timing, the show's just ended. Usually the phone rings just when the good part comes on. Either that or my mom calls me to go do something, like have a bath or wash the dishes.

"Hello, Lark, how are you?" It's that guy Milton who called for my mother the other day.

"Mama's sleeping." I'm not even giving him a chance this time to suck up.

"Lark, I'm hurt. How do you know I didn't call to speak to *you*?"

Save it for the next chump, buddy, 'cause I'm still not buying.

"Why would you be calling to speak to me?" I say. "I don't even know you."

Milton chuckles. "Your mother's told me what a smart kid you are." Then he asks to speak to her.

I say again that she's sleeping. He asks again to speak to her, c'mon Lark, be nice.

"No, I'm not waking her up just to talk on the phone."

I guess I say it a little loud 'cause the next thing I hear is my mother yelling from the top of the stairs, *"Lark, who you talking to on that phone?!"*

I yell up, *"Mama, it's that guy who called you asking for a date the other day!"*

Milton says, "Is that your mother? I thought you said she was sleeping."

Mama yells, *"Who, Milton?!"*

I yell, *"He won't stop asking me to get you!"*

Milton says, "Let me speak to her."

Mama yells, *"Well, tell him I'm trying to sleep!"*

I yell, *"I already did that!"*

Milton says, "C'mon, honey, let me speak to your mother."

Mama yells even louder, *"MILTON!"*

Milton says, "Hey, *Dexter*! Lark, was that your mother calling me?"

I say, "Yeah."

Mama yells, *"Milton, I'm trying to sleep! Let the child get off the phone. I'll talk to you later!"*

I say to Milton, "Did you hear that?"

Milton says, "What did she say?"

I yell, *"Mama, he didn't hear you!"*

Milton says, "C'mon, Lark, don't be like that. Let me speak to her!"

I say, "No!"

I hear Mama grumble loudly and then stomp from the top of the stairs to her room. A second later she picks up her phone and says, "Milton, did the child not tell you I was sleeping? What are you doing? Call me back later." Her words sound like she's mad but her voice has kind of a smile to it.

Milton says, "Hey, I missed you. I just wanted to say hello."

I say, "Mama, tell him you're sleeping and can't talk to him right now."

Both Milton and Mama say, "Lark, get off the phone."

I glance over at the TV. Another show has started, Looney Tunes. Right now Porky Pig is being chased by a ghost.

The doorbell rings. I tell Mama and she says, "Well, go answer it then."

Hmmph.

I put the phone down reluctantly and answer the door. A man in a pair of dark glasses and a gray uniform is standing there grinning. He's got a package under his arm and a notepad in his hand. He says, Hello, little girl, and then he asks if my mother is home. I say she's on the phone. He says, Well, he's got a package here he needs her to sign for so could I please go fetch her, such a cute little girl, run along now.

I scowl at the man and go back to the phone, tell Mama the mailman wants her to come and sign his stinky little notepad. I hear her actually laughing on the phone.

She comes down and as she greets the mailman she picks up the kitchen phone and rests it between her ear and her shoulder. She takes the notepad from the mailman and asks where to sign. I stand between Mama and the mailman as he points out the spot. Mama lingers over the notepad while talking into the phone, saying, "Look, I can't go out with you now. How many different ways can I say the same thing, Milton?" Raising her voice just a little, but still smiling.

I look from my mother's face to the mailman's. He's listening to Mama, waiting for her to sign the notepad. We look at each other.

I shrug my shoulders.

He shrugs his.

Finally Mama clues in and signs the notepad, handing it back to the mailman, who hands her the letter and winks at me as he walks back to his truck.

Mama is still talking to Milton as she opens the letter. I sit down at her feet and keep looking up at her, waiting impatiently for her to hang up, thinking if I send Milton enough hate vibes maybe he'll feel them through the phone. But it doesn't seem to be working 'cause, look, they're still talking!

Mama's talking and reading, reading and talking...she's slowing down, reading a little more now...now she's not saying anything. Her lips are moving...her eyes are starting to get watery...

My mother puts her hands up to her mouth, wipes her eyes, says to Milton, "I'm sorry, I...I'll call you back later."

She hangs the phone up and walks away. I get up. I'm scared. I want to find out what's wrong.

As I'm walking by the phone I turn the ringer off so we won't hear Milton just in case he calls back.

Mama's sitting down in the living room. On the TV Wile E. Coyote is falling off a cliff and when he hits the ground this little cloud of dust rises.

I sit down in front of Mama and look up at her. She's really crying, not even trying to hold it in. I decide to stop looking at her. I know if it was me I wouldn't want someone sitting there staring at me. I'm looking at the floor when I feel Mama's hand on my shoulder. I lift my head, and she's wiping the tears and the snot from her face.

She hands me the letter she was reading. Most of it doesn't make any sense to me, but I understand enough to figure out the letter is to tell Mama that her divorce from Daddy is now final.

Suddenly I'm sad, too. Mama and Daddy haven't lived together for a long time but I guess I still think of them as together. I guess I was always hoping that the two of them might get back together some day, but that's never going to happen, is it.

I try to hug Mama, and at first she doesn't seem to want me to, but then she opens her arms a little and lets me in. She's not crying so much now, just a few tears, and she keeps sniffing up her snot.

She says, "Look at me. Look at how I'm...I mean, I knew it was coming, I don't..."

"Do you still love Daddy, Mama?"

I'm expecting her to say yes. Of course she's going to say yes. Why else would she be crying?

She says, "Oh, my God, no, not at all."

Huh?

She says, "No, baby, my feelings of love for your father died...a *long* time ago. The man I loved is gone. I don't even know who your father is any more."

What does she mean, she doesn't know who he is any more?

"Then why are you crying?" I ask.

Mama sighs. "Lark, I don't know if you can understand this. Your father and I...when we first got together we had so many dreams. We were going to build a home and a family together.... For whatever reason, after you came along those dreams sort of fell apart, and that's not your fault, it just happened. Your father changed. Maybe he feels I changed, too. I know your father's not the same man I loved but I suppose there's still a part of me that remembers and cherishes those dreams we had, and now I have to accept that those dreams are dead....Do you understand what I'm talking about, Lark?"

I nod. I don't know what else to do. I'm not really sure what she's talking about.

I say, "Why does that Milton guy keep calling?"

"He can be sorta pushy, can't he?"

"He gives me the creeps. Are all men like that?"

Mama laughs. "Most of them, yeah. Oh, don't let Milton give you the creeps, Lark. He can't hurt you."

I curl up in Mama's lap and we watch the television for a while. Right now Pepé Le Pew is grabbing some girl skunk and trying to kiss her, and even though she keeps trying to push him away, he won't give up.

Mama says, "You know, Lark, I think I agree with what you said to me the other day. Men are nothing but trouble. All my life—boys, men—if I'd just avoided them things would have been so much easier for me. Not one of them ever proved to be worth my time and effort and I'm starting to think maybe I should just stop dealing with them altogether. No more boys."

No more boys.

"The worst were the ones that I wanted to hate but couldn't because there was just something about them. Ah, you don't even know what I'm talking about, do you? Forget it."

Tears start coming down Mama's face again but she doesn't wipe them up. I'm looking at the people on the TV and then looking at Mama and thinking that no matter how bad things look on TV, no matter if someone gets chased by a ghost or falls off a cliff or dies in a car accident, things always seem kind of nice, and by the end of the show everything's better again.

Mama blows her nose. Tomorrow this time she'll still be sad.   ♦

The sun is going down and I've come home from hanging out at Argy's house all day. I didn't want to go out. I wanted to stay home and take care of Mama but she told me, No, it's a beautiful day, don't waste it. Then she pushed me out the door and into the sunlight, and she was right. It was a beautiful day.

Argy and me tried to hook up with Jennifer but she was gone to her aunt's house so we just did our own thing which was too bad because I was busting to tell Argy my great new idea, but I couldn't. It's too big. All three of us had to be there, especially Jennifer. Her treehouse is a big part of it.

Argy kept wanting to go out but I convinced her we could have fun just hanging around at her place. I didn't want to be outside today. I didn't want to run into Skip the Motorboy.

All day long I've been thinking about my mother crying. When I told Argy, she couldn't believe it. She was like, "No way! *Your* mom? She's too tough. She'd never cry over anything." But it happened.

I unlock our front door and walk in. The house is silent. I look for Mama in the kitchen, the living room and the basement but she's nowhere around, so I walk quietly up the stairs and head for her bedroom. From the hallway I can see her standing out on her balcony. I go to the door and watch her.

She looks so beautiful standing there. It looks like she's just gotten out of the shower. Her hair looks wet, there are drops of water on her shoulders, and she's wearing a tank top like she usually does after she's finished drying herself. Her long dreads are blowing gently in the breeze and she has her hands in her hair, playing with it, separating it, like she's letting the air dry it. She turns her head slightly to the side and I see she has her eyes closed, her head held up high and proud.

She looks so much better than she did this morning, I almost forget she was crying. It was weird to see her like that. I'm not used to it. It's like Argy said. My mother is tough, nothing can hurt her.

How could Daddy do this to her? How could he make her cry like she did? And then there's that Milton guy. What does he want? Would he hurt her if he could?

I think about Skip the Motorboy. I think, how could I have been so stupid? That whole kiss thing. I must have been out of my mind! What if he tells someone? What if someone saw? I could just say he was lying if he says something but what do I say if someone saw?

Boys are evil creatures.

◆

The next day I'm returning from an errand my mother sent me on to the corner store when I hear my name. I turn around and it's the Motorboy calling me, saying, Lark, hey, I haven't seen you in forever. Where you been?

I let him skate up to me, big smile on his face, and before he can say anything I pull his skateboard out from under him and as he falls to the ground and bounces on his bum, I stick my tongue out at him and walk away.

8 | The No-Boys Club

"Let the first meeting of the No-Boys Club come to order," I say, standing at the front of Jennifer's treehouse, sounding as much like an adult as I can. I look at my recruits, my disciples—so far only Jennifer and Argy, but that'll be changing real soon. Argy's her usual happy self but Jennifer looks bored. She doesn't understand the importance of what we're doing, but she will. I'll make sure of that.

"HEY!" I yell, just to get their attention. They both jump. Now Jennifer's paying attention, looking at me a little suspicious, maybe a little scared.

I say, "The first order of business is to officially, uh, *assume* our places in this organization. First, I'm your president, you know me, you love me, Lark Farragut. I'm also gonna be the...the *recruitment* officer. Jennifer, since your dad built this treehouse, and this will be our official HQ, I'm gonna make you *vice*-president and co-recruitment officer. Sorry,

Argy, it's nothing personal, I'm sure you would have done a great job."

Argy says, "That's okay."

Jennifer says, "How come you get to be the president?"

"'Cause I made the club up, it was *my* idea. Hey, I'm making you vice-president. What more do you want?"

"*I* should get to be the leader. It's my treehouse."

"You don't even know what we're doing here and you want to be the leader?" She shuts up, and I get back to it. "Argy, I'm making you treasurer and morale officer."

I was talking to my mother about this and she suggested some things I could make Argy and Jennifer. She said that the recruitment officer got people to join and the morale officer kept everybody happy so they'd want to stay, and I thought Argy'd be great at that 'cause she's always got such a good way about her, never really seems to get too down.

Argy's response: *"Cool!"*

"Jennifer, you and me are gonna be responsible for getting other people to join the club. You're good with people. I know you can get people interested in what we're doing."

"I don't even *know* what we're doing."

But I'm too excited to let Jennifer's sulkiness bring me down. For a while, in the back of my head, I've known there's something I've wanted to do that would blow everybody away, but I didn't know what it was.

The other day, after Mama got those divorce papers, it started to come together. Something Mama said stuck in my brain. She said, *No more boys.* I started thinking about all the bad stuff boys do and get away with all the time. Like last year, when Melvin Gilbert let that stink bomb go in Mr. Manish's class and then let Lucy Conway get blamed for it. *I* even thought it was her who did it until I found out it was Melvin, which was stupid 'cause no girl ever laid a stink bomb, and especially not Lucy Conway.

Or like when that Gary guy and his two buddies got caught reading dirty magazines at an assembly, I thought they should have gotten suspended or at least a nice long detention but nothing happened, and I'll bet if a girl ever did something like that she'd be expelled.

Or like Skip making me kiss him, like that Milton guy calling all the time, like Daddy making Mama cry...

I thought, maybe I'm the only one who sees what boys are all about. And if that was true, then I had to do something about it. I didn't mean kill them all, although it was kind of a neat idea. I just meant maybe move 'em off to an island or something. Construct a huge boat and sail them off into the ocean, pile 'em into a giant spaceship and fly them to the moon. Build all the boys a big moon city and have them live there, and we'll take the earth and it'll be a beautiful, wonderful place again.

My mother laughed with joy when I told her. She asked if we could keep a few men around, just to do the work and to help make babies. I thought about it and said, okay, maybe a few. I had to admit to myself that I'd like to keep my father.

Mama thought it was a great idea but maybe a little big. She said, "Why don't you start small and work your way up?"

So I came up with something else. If I couldn't blast the boys off to the moon by myself, maybe I could convince them to leave on their own.

I lay the plan out to Jennifer and Argy. "Girls, we have a chance to do something here that people will talk about for centuries. What I'm talking about is a campaign of terror against the boys.

We're gonna use their own tactics against them. We're gonna scare the hell out of them. We're going to give them such a hard time they're gonna run for the hills!"

Jennifer and Argy don't really know what I'm talking about exactly, and neither do I, but here's me really getting into it now, making it up as I go along. Even Jennifer's eyes are starting to light up a bit, but she almost kills it by saying, "That all sounds like fun and everything, but there's only one problem. I kind of *like* boys."

My poor brainwashed sister.

She says, "I'm serious. I think some boys are really cool. I don't want to see my father or my little brother scared off to outer space, and I don't think my mother would be too happy with me if I was the one that did the scaring."

I smile and tell her about keeping a few males around to do the work and to help make babies.

Argy says, "Can we have secret meetings and stuff?"

"Argy, they're *all* going to be secret," I say. "We can't let the boys know what's going on. They might try to send spies in. They might try to break us up, or worse, try to take over, make it a No-*Girls* Club."

Jennifer says, "We should make up names for ourselves, like the Sailor Scouts, and make costumes. My mom knows how to sew real well. We could call ourselves the...the Sailor *Scouters*—"

I say, "We can't call ourselves that, it's the exact name as Sailor Scout. All you did was stick an *er* at the end—"

"Well, how about—"

Wait a second, this is supposed to be *my* club. I make Jennifer vice-president and all of a sudden she wants to assume command.

I say, "Look, we can worry about that stuff later. This is still the first meeting. Right now what we have to worry about is getting new members and planning our first terror campaign. We have a lot of work ahead of us, divas."

As soon as I say the word "work," both Argy and Jennifer's faces drop. What do they think, this club is just supposed to be for fun? This is serious business!

So I remind them of Melvin Gilbert and his stink bomb, of that Gary guy and his dirty mag. I tell them about Milton and my mama crying, and even though I conveniently forget to mention what happened with Skip, by the time I'm finished,

Jennifer and Argy wouldn't touch a boy with a ten-foot pole.

We decide to end the first ever meeting of the No-Boys Club. As we're leaving the treehouse, Argy asks, "Does this mean we have to move Robby Roastbeef off to outer space, too?"

I *knew* she liked him. "Sorry, kid, but it does." I put my arm around her shoulders. "You wouldn't have been happy with a guy named Roastbeef anyway."

Walking down the sidewalk, Jennifer and Argy and me are goddesses, holding our heads high. People clear out of our way as we pass them. Boys flee to the other side of the road, and I sleep well that night because I know that what we're doing is just and noble and right.

9 | Silent but Deadly

A rgy and Jennifer meet me at my house and we go through some of the stuff left over from my birthday party—one or two supplies we'll need for the No-Boys Club. They both show up with ski masks and backpacks, just like I told them.

"What are we doing with ski masks in the middle of summer?" says Jennifer.

I try to explain to her what we'll need them for but when I'm done all she can say is, "I don't wanna wear it. It's too hot."

Cry baby. "You'll need it, trust me," I say.

"And I don't wanna wear the backpack. It's too heavy."

"Jennifer, there's nothing inside it yet."

"Yeah, but there will be."

What was I thinking making this girl vice-president. She's completely useless. But then Argy steps in as the morale officer and tells Jennifer don't worry about it, it'll be great fun, and before you know it Jennifer's smiling and saying okay. I look at Argy, impressed. I made the right choice with her. Hmm...maybe I should promote *her* to co-vice-president.

Once our backpacks are set up I say, "Ready, girls?" We look at each other and then tear down the stairs for the front door.

"Oh, don't you girls look cute," Mama says as I stop to give her a kiss, her looking at us ready for action in our shorts and backpacks.

"We gotta go, Mama," I say, running out the door and down the street.

The last words I hear from her are, "Make sure you girls don't get up to any trouble."

◆

No one is safe from the No-Boys Club.

The fat kid walks down the street. Looks like he's just loafing around alone. What, no friends?

Closer now...oh, it's *Harold*. Stupid guy, lives around the neighborhood. Most of the other kids avoid him. He's walking around with his head in the clouds, not paying any attention. He's wearing shorts, which should make this easier...

Closer now...there's a group of girls a few feet down the sidewalk coming toward Harold. Perfect.

I get to offer him the Skip experience...

Harold stops and, oh, fantastic, he bends over to look at something on the ground...

I run up behind him and yank down his shorts as hard as I can.

"HEY!" Harold screams, as he trips head first to the sidewalk. I've grabbed so hard I've even managed to pull down his underwear so there's Harold, lying on the ground now with his business all over the place.

At first those girls jump back. No one knows what's going on, but when they see Harold's business out, they start laughing hysterically, pointing at it.

Harold's face is bright red. He's stunned. He just sits there looking up at them. He doesn't even realize I'm there. I yell, *"No boy is safe from the No-Boys Club,"* but as he looks up, all he sees is a kid running away wearing a ski mask.

I run back to Argy and Jennifer hiding in the bushes and take off my mask, which feels a little awkward since I have to wear it over my glasses. The three of us are laughing as much as those girls standing over Harold.

Finally I wheeze out, "See, divas? There's nothing to be scared of at all. You hit 'em fast, you surprise 'em, and by the time they realize what's going on you've already done your damage and are running away, and all they see is some girl in a ski mask. They got no idea *what's* going on."

Jennifer says, "You were amazing."

"It was just like that with Skip, girls, exactly."

Argy says, "That looked like *so* much fun."

"It was. Now it's your turn, girls. Are you ready to get the boys?"

Jennifer and Argy both scream, *"YEAH!"*

◆

They started putting this building up last summer. I remember watching them drive all these trucks full of big heavy equipment and start digging a huge hole in the ground. They put a fence around the site and there's even supposed to be a guard who patrols the grounds but no one's ever seen him. Kids sneak in here all the time and mess around, play war games, run up and down the huge hills of dirt, play on the machinery and sometimes even go inside the building that's starting to come up now, finally, after a whole year.

When we spotted the group of boys hopping over the fence with their super soakers, I knew we'd found our next targets. We sneak over the fence and crawl up to the top of a dirt hill, looking down at the boys who've gathered at the bottom of the hill and are running around spraying each other, playing soldiers.

So they like water, huh?

They've broken off into two groups. One group takes off behind a hill.

I signal the divas to put on our ski masks.

We open our backpacks.

"Ready?" I say.

They nod.

We stand up and without warning start throwing water bombs down at the group of boys. My mom had a ton of balloons left after my birthday party and I knew they'd come in handy in our fight against the boys.

And they're getting soaked! One bomb explodes on a kid's head and sprays his friend beside him. Another explodes in a kid's gut and sends him crashing to the dirt. They're dripping but they're so shocked they have no idea what's going on, and before they can look up we duck down again, trying hard not to giggle.

"Hey, what gives?!" one of the boys yells.

"No fair, you guys. The game hasn't even started yet!" another one says. They seem to think it was the other group who soaked 'em.

I guess the boys that took off around the hill hear them yelling because they come back, and immediately the guys we soaked are on them, yelling stuff like, you cheated, no fair, you're supposed to just use the soakers, no one said anything about water bombs!

One of the fellas says, "What are you talking about? We didn't throw any water bombs."

But before anything else is said, the three of us stand up and screech and start throwing the rest of our bombs at the boys. They're ambushed. They're caught like fish in an aquarium, cornered in by the hills surrounding them, so we drill 'em with wave after wave of water bombs and look at 'em running around trying to find a way out.

Argy and Jennifer are really into it. I can't see their faces but I can just imagine their expressions.

I throw the last one and it hits some kid smack in the face! I yell, *No boy is safe from the No-Boys Club!* I watch them standing there looking up at us with fear in their eyes, before I turn and run down the hill, Jennifer and Argy following me.

•

"Let's not overdo it," I say. "It's been a great first day. Why don't we do, say, one more pants-pulling and leave it at that for today?"

Argy and Jennifer both say they want to do the pants pulling, so I say, hey, go for it.

We find some bushes to hide in. From our hiding spot we see a kid walking toward us on the sidewalk with what looks like a grocery bag under his arm, but it's really hard to tell from inside the bushes.

We come up with a plan quickly. As soon as he gets close, I'll jump out of the bushes and startle him. Before he gets a chance to react, both Argy and Jennifer are to come up behind and do the deed. If he's wearing a belt or something like that—well, to be honest we haven't come up with anything yet, but whatever, we'll just wing it.

The boy comes closer. I tell Argy and Jennifer to get in position and they take off a few feet away.

We wait.

The boy is almost in position. I glance over at Argy and Jennifer. Jennifer looks fine but Argy looks sort of concerned. Whatever, my mind's on other things. I'm imagining the scared look on the boy's face when I spring out at him, when I deliver my line about how no boy is safe from us, how he's going to look down on the ground with his pants around his ankles...

I hear Argy saying, "Hey, Lark, *wa*–" but I've already started jumping out of the bushes. I can already see the boy recoiling at the sight of me. I can already feel my heart racing. I can already see...

Skip's face.

Oh, my God, it's Skip. It's *SKIP*, and we're standing there staring at each other and even though he can't see my face 'cause it's covered with a ski mask, I can already hear him saying, *"Lark? Lark, is that you?"* And now I'm backing away and now I'm running away and now I'm jumping into the bushes, and you know what? I'm laughing. I don't know why, I can't help it, but I'm laughing.

◆

The stars are out and we can hear the crickets all the way up in Jennifer's treehouse. We wanted to have a sleepover tonight, and when we asked our parents they all said sure. Jennifer's mom made us a huge dinner and let us take it up to the treehouse. Then after dinner I got a good idea.

We asked Jennifer's father if he had any paint that would be good for painting on material and he said he did. He had all different kinds of colors and he said we could have fun with them, so we took the paints and a bunch of brushes up to the tree-house and started painting No-Boys Club logos on our ski masks and backpacks. Each one was different. Jennifer's was a boy's face inside a circle, with an X drawn through it. Argy's was just the words NO-BOYS CLUB done with little flowers, and I came up with a picture of a boy falling off a skateboard with the club name at the bottom.

Later on we got into our sleeping bags and read from this book of ghost stories that Jennifer got from her brother called *Tales for the Midnight Hour.* Halfway through a story called "The Ten Claws," Argy got scared and begged Jennifer to stop reading. She kept looking out the window and telling us she saw a creature like in the story slinking through the bushes, which was stupid but I wasn't sorry when Jennifer stopped reading because I thought I saw it, too.

Argy kept going on after that about how she'd never be able to sleep, so we joined our sleeping bags together to make one big blanket and huddled together, and in five minutes she was snoring like a walrus.

Me and Jennifer stayed up talking, mostly about what we'd done today, laughing about Skip being the boy whose pants they nearly pulled down. She asked me why I took off when I saw it was Skip, and I told her almost the whole truth. I said I just got surprised to see someone I knew. Amazingly Jennifer let it go at that. Maybe she was just too tired to make more of a fuss.

Then she asked me a question. "Lark, aren't we acting just like boys? Jumping out of bushes and scaring them and pulling their pants down and attacking them and all that. I mean, it was fun, but isn't that the kind of stuff they always do that we get mad at them for?"

I said, "Yeah, but if you don't play the game their way they won't listen to you."

That was about an hour ago. I'm still awake now, just lying here in the dark...

◆

In my dream Skip and I are holding hands, walking toward our neighborhood pool. All of our friends are there but we don't pay any attention to them. We dive into the water together and roll around like dolphins. Holding our breath underwater we kiss, and we decide to never go above water again...

For the first few minutes after I wake up I can't remember the dream. It just feels like a really good night's sleep. I'm smiling but I'm also a little sad. I have this feeling like I've lost something that I really cared about. I don't really know what I'm feeling, and I...

OH, MY GOD!

I was kissing Skip. I remember. I had a dream I was kissing the Motorboy!

Bad enough I did in real life, but now I'm dreaming about it.

For a second I think that everybody knows, that they were all there watching and making fun of me kissing Skip underwater, but I calm down. It was just a dream. I'm still here in Jennifer's treehouse. Both the divas are still asleep beside me, dreaming their own dreams. Nobody knows anything.

But what if they find out? Not about the dream kiss, but about the *real* kiss?

What if Skip opens his big mouth? You know how boys are. They brag about everything, even if it's not true. By now he's probably told everyone he knows.

If anyone finds out...

I'm in a panic. I don't know what to do or what to think. All I do know is that I don't want to think about Skip any more.

But I do keep thinking about him. And I'm *afraid* of why I think I might be thinking about him, of why I might be dreaming about him.

Maybe I...maybe I just...*like* him.

AARRGGHHH. It can't be that!

If anybody found out about this I'd never live it down. After all the things I said about him, about all boys, they'd kick my little behind out of the No-Boys Club so fast...

Ugh...*relax*, stupid...relax.

It was just a *dream.*

No one knows and no one's going to know.

10 | Everybody's Doing What They Want to Do, Not What I Want Them to Do

Okay, I admit it. I have a crush on Skip the Motorboy.

I don't even understand how it happened. He was always just this goofball to me, and now this. Well, fine. I've said it and now I'm never saying it again. I'm going back to the No-Boys Club like nothing ever happened.

Boys have done a lot of really scummy things to a lot of people. How can I feel like I do about this guy if he's one of them? They lie and they cheat and they make people cry. My mother's said it herself. She's gotta know what she's talking about. She wouldn't say it if it weren't true.

I open my front door at the sound of the doorbell and I'm surprised to see that Argy and Jennifer have brought Xan and Laura with them.

"Hey, Laura, hey, Xan," I say. "How you doing? I haven't seen you guys since my party."

Laura and Xan both say hi. Then Jennifer jumps in, saying, "C'mon, we're going over to my treehouse."

I'm not really dressed so I tell them I have to get ready and I'll meet them later. When I close the door I realize I'm feeling jealous. I guess I think of the treehouse as *our* treehouse—I mean mine and Argy's and Jennifer's. Why's she gotta invite those two over?

Twenty minutes later I'm climbing up the tree-house ladder. I hear laughter coming from inside and that jealousy comes back at me, stronger this time.

When Jennifer sees me coming inside she jumps up all excited.

"Guess what," she screams. "Xan and Laura are gonna join our club! Isn't that great?"

Yeah, I guess...

Jennifer says, "I was at the mall with my mom this morning and I saw them at Wal-Mart and I was telling them about all the cool stuff we did with the ski masks and the water bombs and all that and they were getting really excited and then I, like, asked 'em to join and they were jumping up and down, saying *yeah*—"

Now Jennifer's jumping up and down. But somehow I'm not nearly as thrilled by this news as I should be.

Xan says, "Oh, man, Lark, it sounds like a really great club. You know, getting back at the boys and everything. Girl Power. I wish you'd told us about it sooner. I would have loved to be there when you guys bombed those guys at the construction site!"

Laura chimes in with pretty much the same song and dance, real excited by the club and really anxious to join.

"You really wanna join?" I say, sort of hoping they'll say no.

"Are you kidding?" Xan says. "I can't wait. I got a ski mask I could use. It's got holes in it but it's still good."

This goes on and on. They're jabbering away and even though when I first started the club this is exactly what I wanted, now that people are starting to get interested I'm just not thrilled like I should be. I look at Xan and Laura and start getting upset that they're here, wanting them to just go and I don't understand why 'cause they're my friends.

I say, "I don't know if you two should join. I mean, it's really hard and we have a lot to do and I don't know if you'd be any good at this."

Laura says, "What do you mean? I'll be great. I really want to join, Lark."

Jennifer says, "Yeah, what's your problem, Lark?"

"I don't have any problem. I'm just saying, that's all. What's *your* problem, Jennifer?"

"*You're* my problem."

Next thing I know, Laura and Xan are giving me attitude, saying they can join the club if they want to. I say no they can't, it's *my* club, I'm the only one who gets to say if people can join or not. Laura says, No, Jennifer already said they can join so I can't say anything, and then she starts going, Right, Jennifer? Right, Jennifer? Looking at her, trying to get her to talk.

I start getting supermad. I can't control my voice. It's all wavery feeling and the only way to stop it from doing that is by yelling, and pretty soon I can't even control that. I'm screaming at everyone, going, *"No, you can't join. It's my club. I'm the one who made it up so I'm the leader and I say you can't join so you can't! Why don't you get your own club? Why do you have to be a part of mine?! You should have told me you were inviting them in, Jennifer. You shouldn't have done it without telling me, you should have asked me first!!!"*

I hear Jennifer yell, "*You're* the one that said I was supposed to get new people to join, stupid head," but my back is turned as she says it. I'm stomping across the treehouse to the ladder, climbing down, running away.

♦

When I left the treehouse I didn't let them see but I was almost crying. I was fighting to stop the tears from coming, wiping away tears that weren't even there.

But now, instead of crying, I'm so mad I don't know what to do with myself. I know I don't want to go home. My mother's going to ask what's wrong. I won't be able to hide it from her and I just don't want to talk about it right now.

I wander around aimlessly for a while. I go down to the creek where me and Skip played that time but when I get there I see a bunch of kids walking by the water and I decide not to go down after all. I want to go to the store where Skip and me took those money-back bottles, but I don't have any money so I don't bother.

Walking around, walking, walking...

What am I doing? There's nothing to do out here. I might as well go home.

If Jennifer or any of them call me, I'm not gonna answer the phone. I'm not talking to them again. I want a big, *big* apology. Maybe if Argy calls I'll speak to her, but that's it.

Before I go home I find myself walking down Skip's street. I walk by his house on the other side of the street and look up into what I think is his window and before I really realize it I'm stopping and wondering what he's doing now, if he's even home.

I walk down the street a bit but then I stop. I cross to the side of the street Skip's house is on and I walk by it again, but this time I don't look up in the window all that long.

I decide to walk home.

◆

Mama and I are sitting in the kitchen eating dinner when she says, "So happy you could find the time to join your mother for dinner, Lark. Since you started your club I barely see you."

When I came home I think Mama could tell I was upset, but I guess she figured I didn't want to talk about it, so she let me go up to my room and left me alone until dinner was ready.

Mama says, "How's things going with your club there, Baby Lark?"

So I tell her. And then I start crying. Mama comes around to my seat and puts her arms around me and I hug her hard and bury my head in her chest. She starts caressing my neck and hair and back and tells me it's okay, let it out, and I cry for a few more minutes 'cause I don't know how to stop.

Pretty soon I start to calm down. Mama gives me a Kleenex and I blow my nose and wipe the tears off my face.

Mama says, "That was quite a session of tears. You feel better, baby?"

I nod.

Mama says, "So, let me make sure I understand you. You feel that your friends went behind your back by inviting those two other girls into your club. You feel they should have told you first before they did that. Is that more or less it, Lark?"

I nod. But somehow when she says it, it doesn't feel the way it did at the treehouse.

"Well, I agree, if your friends went behind your back, that's a pretty bad thing. A friend shouldn't do that to another friend. But, baby, didn't you say to Jennifer that you *wanted* her to get new people to join? Wasn't she just doing what you told her to do in the first place?"

I nod.

"Okay, well, if that's so, then why do you feel like your friends betrayed you? And Xan and Laura *are* your friends, aren't they? Weren't they here at your birthday party?"

I nod.

"It sort of sounds to me like you've gotten used to things going a certain way—*your* way basically, and maybe you feel a little threatened by Xan and Laura coming in. Maybe you feel like things are going to change. Would that be fair to say?"

I nod. I don't want to but I nod. That is how I feel.

Mama says, "That's a perfectly natural way to feel, baby, but Jennifer and Argy love you. They wouldn't go behind your back. You girls have to stick together. It's a hard world out there for you sometimes. I mean, Lark, I'm really impressed with you. You've been able to gather people around you and create something really great. Why not take some pride in that and have some fun with it? Surely there must be room for a couple of other girls in your club, isn't there?"

I nod. I feel stupid over the way I acted. I feel like a brat, but I don't want to admit it. Why should I admit it?

I start to settle down a little. Mama sees this and starts to ruffle my hair a little and snarfs my neck. I don't want to but I can't hold it in. I giggle.

Mama giggles, too. She takes my glasses off and tries to put them on her face. Too small. She says, "Is there anything else you want to talk to me about, kid?"

I get kind of squirrely. I turn my head and try to hold back a little grin.

"C'mon, I saw that. Spill it. Seriously, if there's anything you want to talk to me about, Lark, I want to hear it. I promise I won't laugh. C'mon, girl, I know you want to tell me."

Actually I don't. I'm embarrassed, but the words start coming out of me anyway.

Mama doesn't quite laugh out loud. But she's got this big ol' grin on her face. She's looking at me with that oh-that's-so-*cute* face, and I immediately regret that I've just told her how I've been feeling about Skip, but hey, look, there's my lips still flapping, still telling her about him. I tell her about the creek and buying junk food with him and flying down the sidewalk on his skateboard and the dream. What I *don't* tell her about is the kiss.

Mama picks me up and puts me on her lap. She says, "Lark, maybe you have a crush on him."

Ugghhh! I *know* I've got a crush on him. I want you to tell me I *don't* have a crush on him, Mama!

"What's the matter? Don't you want to have a boyfriend?"

NO, I *don't* want a boyfriend!

I sputter, "Boys, they're...they're bad, they're rotten, they're evil, they—"

Mama looks at me, amused, but also a little shocked. "Lark, where did you get all this?" she asks.

"From you," I say. "You're always talking about how men are no good, always saying bad stuff about them. You even say bad stuff about Daddy, and you were married to him. And just a little while ago you said that girls need to stick together."

"Oh, Lark, Lark..." Mama looks a little concerned. "Baby...of *course* it's important that girls stick together, but that doesn't mean you have to hate boys to do it. Just because you find a boy attractive doesn't mean that suddenly you're bailing out on your girlfriends, Lark. This boy'll be one friend, and your girlfriends will still be your girlfriends. Lark, you have to understand. I have said some bad things about men. I have said some bad things about your father, but you should never take that like I'm saying *all* men are evil or whatever. They're not." She smiles. "A few of them are actually okay, believe it or not."

"But—" I'm not sure what I want to say.

"Listen, I should tell you while we're on the subject of men. I've decided to go out with Milton. You remember Milton."

Yeah, I remember Milton.

I can't believe what I'm hearing. When did *this* happen?

"You remember that day I got the divorce papers? Well, Milton wound up calling me that night. I was still crying. I don't know why I picked up the phone, but it was him and he asked me what was wrong and I told him and he was really great. He just listened to me, you know, he really listened, and then later he said some things to me that really helped because he went through a similar situation with his ex-wife. I don't know, Lark, I just saw a different side to the guy. So about a week later when he asked me out I said okay."

I get off Mama's lap and sit down again in my seat. "So what's gonna happen now? You gonna get married to him?"

Mama's face darkens. "Lark, don't be silly. We're just going out. We're just *friends*. Why would you think I'd be getting married to this man? I barely know him."

"Does Daddy know about this?"

I can see Mama getting mad at me but I don't care because I can feel myself getting mad at her.

She says, trying not to shout, "Now why would I tell your father? Huh, Lark? What possible reason would I have to do that? Why is it every time I make a decision you have to know if I cleared it with your father first? Your father is *your* father, he's not mine. I don't have to check anything with him. I don't have to tell him *anything* any more, and the sooner you understand that the better."

I burst into tears. They're streaming down my face and I don't even think about stopping them. I think Mama tries to touch me to comfort me but I push her hand away. I hear her say, "Go on up to your room and lie down a while, Lark," but I just sit there crying. I want my father. I want to be at my father's house. I want his arms around me and I ask

Mama, I *tell* Mama I want to go and be with him.

And Mama starts shouting, "Are you out of your mind? You think you're gonna go running to your father every time I do something you don't like? You better get that notion out of your...look, just go on up to your room, Lark. I'll be up there later."

I run up to my room and slam the door. I'm pacing around the room here and there, but I get tired, so I sit down in a corner and I cry. I just cry.

◆

I wait for an apology from Mama that never comes. Me and her don't speak much for the rest of the night and most of the next day. I pretty much stay in my room doing stuff by myself. I don't even watch TV 'cause I don't feel like going downstairs and being around her.

Around dinner time the day after our fight, Mama knocks on my door. I think she's going to tell me to come down and eat but she's standing there holding out the cordless phone she keeps in her room. She hands me the phone and says, "Your father wants to talk to you." Then she heads downstairs.

"Hello, Daddy?" I say.

"Hey, Lark," he says. "Your mother called me.

She tells me the two of you had some problems last night, that you wanted to speak to me."

I'm surprised that she called him after what she said but I forget that in a second, telling Daddy all about what happened yesterday, about her yelling at me, about her going out with this new guy and not even telling us.

I'm expecting my father to get mad, but he doesn't. Instead he sounds happy. He asks me what this Milton person is like, and what he does for a living, and I tell him he works at the hospital with Mama, but that's all I know. Daddy says that's great, that he's happy that she's going out with someone, that he hopes Milton is a nice guy and that they have a really good time together. He says, "Your mother's a good woman. She deserves to meet someone nice."

Daddy tells me I should be happy that Mama is going to go out and have fun with someone. He asks me, don't I think she's entitled to that, and what can I say, of course I do, I just...

"Your mother's right, Lark," Daddy says. "We're not married any more. She's free to do what she likes. But that has nothing to do with you and me. I'm still your father, you're still my daughter, nothing can change that. Even if she wound up getting married to that guy, he wouldn't become your father. I'd still be your father. I always will be. We'll always belong to each other, baby. Don't be scared about that."

"Daddy, is it my fault that you and Mama aren't together anymore?"

"Sweetpea, how could you say something like that? Of course not."

"Sometimes I think if maybe I was a better daughter, you wouldn't have wanted to get away from me and Mama, we'd still be a family."

I want to put my arms around Daddy, but he's just a voice over the phone, so I press the phone close to my ear and curl up under the covers, putting the sheets over my head and keeping Daddy to myself, my little secret.

11 | Boys and Girls

After I spoke to my father I felt bad about the way I had acted toward my mother. So I told Mama I was sorry and she said she was sorry, too.

I haven't done anything with The No-Boys Club for days. I haven't gone by the treehouse, I haven't talked to Jennifer or Argy, I haven't really even thought much about it, which when I realized it I was really surprised by. Jennifer and Argy called me a couple of times but I didn't much feel like talking to them so I got Mama to tell them I'd call 'em back later. Maybe I will. I'm starting to miss them, to be honest.

On Tuesday Mama went out on her date with that Milton guy. I watched her get ready for it. I watched her take a bath. I watched her pick out clothes to wear. I watched her put a little make-up on her face and I helped her do her hair up nice. She looked beautiful. But it seemed like a lot of trouble to go through just to go out.

That Milton guy came to the house to pick her up. I answered the door and he said, Oh, you must be Lark, I'm so happy to meet you, yadda, yadda, yadda. But he offered me a small box of brownies, and I have to admit that earned him some brownie points. Get it? *Brownie* points?

Mama asked me a million times if I was going to be all right at home by myself and I told her a million times I'd be just fine, that I was a big girl and I knew how to take care of myself. Both Mama and Milton laughed. She said she wouldn't be home late and she'd call me to see how I was doing.

I finished off the brownies in front of the television. When I finished the last one I felt a little queasy, so lazing around in front of the TV for a couple of hours was just what the doctor ordered. Later I went upstairs to draw for a while. Man, I love it when Mama goes out and I get the house to myself. I feel like the queen of the castle. In fact, I was kinda sad when I heard Milton's car pull up and then heard Mama's key in the lock.

She came home in a good mood. She was smiling and talking, said she'd had a really good time. Said she'd probably go out with Milton again some time.

Great.

I went to bed kind of upset that she'd had such a good time with that Milton guy. I knew it was wrong. I didn't want to feel that way after what me and Daddy had talked about, but I couldn't help it.

The next day, today, I went over to Jennifer's house. We looked at each other a little without saying much and then she called Argy and told her to come over.

I didn't want to talk about the No-Boys Club, but of course we wound up getting into it anyway. They said I should lighten up and why'd I get so mad over nothing? I said I was sorry for the way I acted, and then, I don't know, the subject changed and we were arguing about something else, and then we were laughing, can you believe that was Skip you jumped out at from the bushes, I know, can you believe it, whatever, no big deal. We went up to the treehouse for a while, but it got boring so we went out and ran around the neighborhood.

We were the three divas together again. We got soaked by a dog shaking water off itself after running through a sprinkler. We laughed at a group of boys we saw sitting on a curb at the corner store. We sat in the park under a bridge and looked out at the little duck families swimming along and talked about nothing in particular.

The summer had just begun, and for the first time I realized it was almost over. School would be starting next week. I wondered if I'd done enough with my summer but I couldn't really come up with an answer and I forgot about it almost as soon as I thought of it.

Argy had to go home just 'cause her dad said so. Me and Jennifer hung out for a while longer but soon she had to go, too, so we said goodbye and went our separate ways. We'd all see each other again tomorrow.

I didn't feel like going home so I decided to go for a walk.

◆

Who am I fooling?

No one. I guess I'm not even fooling myself any more.

Somehow I manage to drag myself up to his door. I almost turn around a few times but then I just do it. I push the doorbell before I can even think about it.

And no one comes to the door. It feels like hours I'm waiting there, terrified that someone's actually going to come. I have enough time to think, what am I doing here, but I don't have enough time to leave because suddenly I hear the door opening, and a large man is standing there looking at me.

I swallow hard. "Is...is Skip home?"

The large man grins down at me. He says, "Yeah, he's in. Would you like to come in, honey?"

I step inside. The large man walks to a door that must lead to the basement and yells into it, *"Herschel! Come on upstairs. Someone's here to see you!"*

Herschel? Holy cow, is that Skip's real name? I can't decide which name is worse.

After a moment I hear movement coming up the stairs.

I hear his voice. "Who is it, Pop?"

I see his face—Skip/Herschel/Motorboy—peeking around the door and seeing me, his face going from curious to not happy.

We look at each other for a moment.

"Hi, Skip."

"Hey, Lark."

Maybe he looks a *little* happy to see me.

◆

Me and Skip are walking down the street. Skip's brought his skateboard, but he's not riding it. He's holding it and walking with me. We're not really saying much.

"Herschel? Is that really your name?" I'm only laughing a little.

"Yeah, that's my name, so what?"

"So, I always wondered what your real name was. I knew there was no way your parents called you no *Skip*." I try to make a joke out of it but Skip's not laughing, and I have to admit, if I had a name like Herschel I probably wouldn't be laughing, either. "I'm just teasing you. Herschel's not such a bad name."

Skip says, "So what do you want, Lark? Come to pull my board out from under me? Or maybe you want to pull my pants down again."

"No, of course I don't."

"I'm not riding my board around you ever again. Every time I do I wind up falling off and bouncing on my ass."

We both laugh a little. I say, "I promise I'll never do that to you again. Cross my heart."

"That's what you say now. Next time, especially if you're gonna pull down my pants, just please make sure there are no people around, okay, and especially no girls..."

"No, the next time I do it, it's going to be at recess so the whole school can see."

"Yeah, and I'm gonna turn around and pull down your *dress* or your pants or whatever you're wearing. I don't care, you wait."

We're both laughing now. "You should have seen you," I say. "You looked so funny lying there on the ground. I wished I'd had a camera, you looked so cute."

Jeez, why say that, so *stupid*...

Skip says, "Yeah, well..." and then we don't say anything for a little while.

We're just standing there on the street, right near one of the neighborhood churches. The sun is starting to go down and I know I should be heading home now. We look at each other stupidly for a couple of seconds and giggle and look away. I touch his shirt and take my hand away.

Skip says, "I was thinking the other night about that time when you kissed me—"

I grab his shirt at the collar and say, "Did you tell anyone about that?" My eyes are locked to his.

"*Hell,* no. I never told. You think I want anyone

knowing your mouth touched mine?" And then he takes my hand off his shirt. He holds on to my hand for a second and it doesn't look like he's going to let it go but then he does.

I say, "So what were you thinking about it?"

"I dunno. I was just thinking."

"Did you like it?"

"I dunno. Did you?"

"Maybe."

"Well, maybe I did, too."

"Do you want to do it again?"

"Maybe. What, right here?"

"No, not right here. Someone might see us."

I point to some bushes near the church and we run there, going deep inside where no one can see.

We look at each other for a full minute. I close my eyes and I tell him to close his. I pucker my lips and move my face closer to his. I feel his lips against mine, pressing lightly. My glasses fog up.

I open my eyes and I see Skip still has his closed, and I close mine again.

When we're done kissing, we look at each other and giggle, but I don't feel the need to run away like I did the last time this happened.

Instead I say, "Look, *Herschel,* if you ever...*ever* tell anyone about what we just did..."

But I don't finish what I'm saying.

I look at Skip smiling at me...

And I smile back.